PUFFIN BOO

LONDON S

Jim Eldridge was born in 1944 in London. He now lives in rural Cumbria with his wife. He has been writing for many years, most of his work being for television and radio. He is an award-winning writer, with over four hundred television and radio scripts broadcast and forty-five books published. His main interests outside writing are organic-vegetable gardening, reading, history and films.

LONDON SIEGE

J. ELDRIDGE

A fictional story
based on real-life events

PUFFIN BOOKS

*To my wife, Lynne, for putting up
with the stress of my research*

PUFFIN BOOKS

Published by the Penguin Group
Penguin Books Ltd, 80 Strand, London WC2R 0RL, England
Penguin Putnam Inc., 375 Hudson Street, New York, New York 10014, USA
Penguin Books Australia Ltd, 250 Camberwell Road, Camberwell,
Victoria 3124, Australia
Penguin Books Canada Ltd, 10 Alcorn Avenue, Toronto, Ontario,
Canada M4V 3B2
Penguin Books India (P) Ltd, 11 Community Centre, Panchsheel Park,
New Delhi – 110 017, India
Penguin Books (NZ) Ltd, Cnr Rosedale and Airborne Roads, Albany,
Auckland, New Zealand
Penguin Books (South Africa) (Pty) Ltd, 24 Sturdee Avenue, Rosebank 2196,
South Africa

Penguin Books Ltd, Registered Offices: 80 Strand, London WC2R 0RL, England

www.penguin.com

First published 2003
1

Copyright © Jim Eldridge, 2003
All rights reserved

Although based on real-life events, all characters in this book are fictional.

The moral right of the author has been asserted

Set in Bookman Old Style

Made and printed in England by Clays Ltd, St Ives plc

British Library Cataloguing in Publication Data
A CIP catalogue record for this book is available from the British Library

ISBN 0–141–31588–1

CONTENTS

HISTORY
OF THE
SAS

WHO DARES WINS

THE HISTORY OF THE SAS

The SAS developed from the Commandos of the British Army during the Second World War. David Stirling was a lieutenant in the Commandos fighting in the deserts of North Africa in 1941. He believed that a small group of men working covertly behind enemy lines could have a devastating effect. His idea was given official approval and so the Special Air Service was born. The newly formed SAS, just sixty-five men strong, carried out its first operation in November 1941, hitting enemy-held airfields on the North African coast. It worked with such effectiveness against the German forces in the deserts of North Africa that, in September 1942, the SAS was raised to full regiment status, 1 SAS Regiment – with a force of 650 men divided into four combat squadrons: A, B, C (the Free French Squadron) and D (the SBS, or Special Boat Section).

In 1943 an additional regiment, 2 SAS, was

created. Both regiments fought in the Allied invasion of Italy and Sicily in 1943, and then took part in the D-Day landings of June 1944, fighting behind enemy lines.

After the end of the Second World War, the SAS was disbanded. However, many ex-SAS men, who had seen the advantages of such a force, lobbied the War Office for its reinstatement in the British Army. The result was that, in 1947, an SAS unit, the Artists Rifles, was formed as part of the Territorial Army. Its official title was 21 SAS (Artists) TA, and many ex-SAS soldiers joined this new outfit. However, the military top brass reduced the SAS in size and importance. Many of the top brass did not like what they considered to be an 'unorthodox organization' within the ranks. By 1949 the SAS consisted of just two squadrons and a signals detachment.

Then, in 1950, came the Malayan conflict. Malaya had been under British control for many years. In 1948 Britain had set up the Federation of Malaya as a step towards independence. However, the minority Chinese population of Malaya, backed by Communist China, resented the domination of the federation by Malay people. Calling themselves the MRLA (Malayan Races Liberation Army), they began a campaign against the British and Malays. During 1950 the MRLA killed 344 civilians and 229 soldiers.

Mike Calvert had fought with Orde Wingate's Chindits behind enemy lines in the Burmese jungle in the Second World War. He had ended the war as Commander of the SAS and he was given the task of reforming it into a fighting unit to deal with the MRLA. In 1950 Calvert set up a force known as the Malaya Scouts (SAS). This was made up of men from B Company, 21 SAS; C Squadron from Rhodesia (now called Zimbabwe), and some reservists. In 1952 the Malaya Scouts became officially known as 22 SAS. 22 SAS fought so successfully behind enemy lines in the jungles of Malaya – living and working with the local peoples – that by 1956 the leaders of the MRLA had fled to Thailand. The Malaya campaign came to an end in 1960, with the SAS having proved itself and its techniques of covert operations.

The strategic structure of an SAS Squadron had now been defined. An SAS Squadron consists of sixty-four men in sixteen four-man troops. Each troop has to be able to operate independently, living off the land. As well as being proficient in every kind of weapon and unarmed combat, the troop is capable of dealing with every possible medical emergency.

Further campaigns followed in which the SAS played a key role. In Aden and Borneo (1959–67) and in Oman (1970), SAS soldiers fought behind enemy lines – gaining the support of the local people and militia, blending into the scenery and attacking the enemy where least expected. During the 1970s and 1980s the SAS were major players in the war against terrorism in Northern Ireland. In 1982 the SAS played an important part in the Falklands War, and in 1991 in the Gulf War against Iraq.

Wherever war or terrorism threatens, the SAS is there.

SELECTION FOR THE SAS

As the SAS's reputation grew, more and more soldiers applied to join this élite unit. Only ten per cent of those who apply pass the tests and are finally selected. Just one in ten. Why the pass rate is so low can be seen from the following, which sets out the rigours of the SAS Selection and Training process.

● Any male who is a member of the Army, Navy or RAF and who is between nineteen and thirty-four years of age can apply to be selected for the SAS.

● After applying, candidates undergo three weeks of endurance trials in the mountainous country of the Brecon Beacons in Wales.

● The trials consist of daily route marches, against the clock, across the wild landscape of the Brecon Beacons, including crawling through ditches filled with filthy water. These marches take place both by day and by night, so adding sleep-deprivation as a factor to the trials.

Candidates will find that their orders are subject to last-minute change, adding to the stress being put on them. "Officer candidates" will also be instructed to plan a commando raid or behind-enemy-lines patrol.

● At the end of the first week, those considered not to be fit enough are RTUd (returned to their own unit). The candidates who pass undergo two more weeks of forced marches through mountainous country. During these two weeks the length of the marches, and the weight of the bergens, are increased every day, as is the pressure on the men.

● During the final week, Test Week, candidates have to march three times up and down Pen-y-fan. At nearly 1,000 metres, this is the tallest mountain in the Brecon Beacons. Each march covers a distance of 30 miles. At any point on this march an instructor can appear and ask a candidate to assemble an unfamiliar weapon, or some other task, such as solving a mathematical problem. In addition, the candidates have to swim across the River Wye, naked but carrying their clothes, their rifle, and their heavy bergen.

● The Final Test is a forty-six-mile endurance course, carrying full bergen weighing twenty-five kilos, which has to be completed in under twenty hours. If the candidate survives this, he is given a weekend break and told to report to Stirling Lines, which is the SAS's base at Hereford. He will then start Continuous Training, which lasts for fourteen weeks.

SAS ENDURANCE TEST KIT LIST

Candidates are issued with the following kit:

- a rucksack known as a bergen
- a poncho for wet-weather protection
- a compass and maps
- two water-bottles (each able to hold one and a half pints of water)
- a brew kit (to make hot drinks)
- three twenty-four-hour ration packs (for the first three days of the test)
- a rifle

On the first day of the trials the candidates have to carry a weight of eleven kilos. By the end of the three weeks the bergens weigh twenty-five kilos.

Chapter 1
HIJACK

Chris fixed the plastic explosive to the outside of the door of the Boeing 737, pressing it hard against the bottom of the door to make sure it would stick, but not so hard that the noise would alert the terrorists inside the plane. There were four terrorists holding twenty-three hostages. Their lives depended on Chris planting the explosive without detection. Chris is Chris Watson, my best mate. Me, I'm Dave Harris. Nineteen years old. We're both troopers with the SAS.

The plane was parked in an isolated part of the airport, far from the terminals and from the glare of floodlights. We'd waited until it was night before we made our move, so that Chris and I could get to the plane without being seen.

From messages coming through the

headphones in our helmets, we knew that two of the terrorists were in the cockpit with the pilots. We weren't exactly sure where the other two were. I hoped they were right by the door so that when we blew it and went in they'd be in our sights. Even with directional microphones aimed at the plane, our controller still couldn't be sure where everyone was. There was only one way to find out, and that was to go in.

There's always that moment of worry before you go in. Not worry about members of the team: we're trained to take care of ourselves. If we get hit, well, that goes with the job. Our main worry is not harming the hostages. The trouble is, in the heat of action, with the air filled with smoke and everything happening in the space of a few seconds, it can be difficult identifying who's a terrorist and who's a hostage. You have to do your best to keep your wits about you – think fast, and act faster.

Chris looked at me through the visor of his gas mask and I gave him a thumbs up. Chris and I ran down the steps and hid under the belly of the plane. Then Chris detonated the plastic.

BOOOOMMM!!

The door tore off its hinges. Even as it did so, Chris and I were up the steps, our machine-guns at the ready. I chucked a flash-bang (stun-grenade) into the cabin of the plane and we both turned our heads away to protect our eyes as it went off. A flash-bang disorientates for up to forty-five seconds, which gives you a real advantage over the enemy.

We went into the cabin. Chris turned sharp left and dived into the cockpit. I heard his machine-gun stutter *tat-tat-tat! tat-tat-tat!* as he let off two bursts. My eyes quickly scanned the cabin and I spotted one of the terrorists half hidden behind a row of seats, just rising up, his gun aimed at me. I let him have it with two rounds.

A movement to my right made me swing round and I was just about to give a burst, when I stopped myself in time. It was one of the hostages, standing up with his hands in the air.

'Down!' I yelled.

Then I saw another terrorist, his coat open and one hand reaching to detonate the bombs strapped round his body.

Tat-tat-tat! Tat-tat-tat! Tat-tat-tat!

The terrorist took all three rounds full in

11

the head and shoulders and fell backwards
out of sight. I looked towards the door to
the cockpit. Chris was just coming out. He
gave a thumbs up.

And that was when our bleepers went
off.

Chapter 2
BRIEFING

Chris and I came down the aircraft steps, taking off our gas masks and helmets as we did so. I checked my bleeper. The message on the display panel said, 'Contact HQ'. Chris held up his bleeper. It said the same.

'Maybe it's some real action instead of this practising,' said Chris.

'Maybe,' I said. 'Mind, that was a good one today.'

The rescue from the 737 had been an exercise, but as frighteningly like the real situation as you could want it to be. With one exception: the hostages and the terrorists were just cardboard cut-outs. Apart from that, everything inside the Killing House was built to be an exact replica of the real thing.

The Killing House at SAS HQ in

Hereford is a huge building with six big rooms, each of which can be made up to look like a terrorist scenario. Today, one of the rooms had been turned into the airliner that me and Chris had practised on. In another room, the control room of a nuclear power station had been recreated. Ships, oil rigs, everything could be simulated inside the Killing House.

As we were already at SAS HQ we went at the double to the Duty Room. There we were told to head straight away for hangar two, where we'd be briefed.

'Hanger two,' grinned Chris. 'Maybe we're flying off somewhere exotic. Somewhere hot.'

'Some stinking jungle where the mosquitoes are big as rats and chew their way through your mosquito net,' I commented.

'Not necessarily,' replied Chris. 'Could be rescuing hostages in Spain. We do the job, and then we have a holiday. Lying on the beach and soaking up the sun.'

That was Chris all over. He loved the beach. His favourite sports were anything to do with the sand and sea – surfing, beach football and volleyball. It showed, too. He was one of those lucky people who tan easily. The sort that those of us who go a spotty pink or a burnt red envy. Not that I could ever really envy Chris. We were too much good mates for that. We'd joined the training course for the SAS at the same time, Chris coming from the Army, me from the Royal Marines.

We'd hit it off after I'd found him up to his neck in a bog in the mountains of Wales. I was soaking wet, stinking and exhausted after running fifteen miles over the Brecon Beacons with a full pack and a rifle. Up till then, all I'd seen of Chris was this tanned guy, about my age, running ahead of me and jumping from rock to rock with the ease of a mountain goat. Look at him! I'd thought bitterly: Tall! Fit! He'll get into the SAS easily, while I'll have to work hard for it. And then suddenly he'd disappeared. One minute he was running and jumping, and the next he was gone.

I'd weighed up in my mind whether just to ignore him and carry on running to complete the twenty-mile course. Maybe he'd just decided to hide and take a rest. Or maybe he'd fallen and broken his leg. I decided to check, so I ran over to where I'd last seen him. And there he was, up to his neck in filthy water in a bog.

'What are you doing in here?' I'd asked. And he grinned up at me and replied, 'Fishing.'

That did it for me. Even though I was dog-tired, I couldn't help laughing. I reached down a hand and said, 'Come on. Out you come!'

I'd helped him struggle out, and then we set off together to finish the run. That had been a year ago.

Lucky for us, we both survived selection for the SAS and the many training courses that followed. Now we were part of the same SAS squad, watching out for each other. You need mates you can depend on when your life is on the line most of the time.

We reached hangar two and found one of our squad, Chocko, already there. We called him Chocko because he had this passion for eating bars of chocolate. Why he wasn't as fat as a balloon, I'll never know. Some people are just like that; they can eat and eat and never grow fat. Other people just have to sniff a chocolate bar and they put on weight. Maybe Chocko was lucky because he was tall – about 6 foot 3 – the tallest bloke in our squad. Chris is next tallest, at 6 feet. Me, I'm 5 feet 10, like most of the others.

Also in the hangar was Captain Mears, and we could tell from the serious expression on his face that something big was in the offing.

'Right, forget the formalities,' said Mears. 'Let's get straight down to business. We've got a problem at the Ajanian Embassy in London.'

Chris and I exchanged looks. So it wasn't to be either a sunny beach in Spain or a tropical jungle: it was London.

'What sort of problem?' asked Chris.

Mears shook his head.

'We don't know. Planning and Intelligence had a tip-off not long ago that something was brewing.'

'Do we know who it came from?' I asked.

'A man called Billy Acres. He's with the guard-dogs section at Heathrow Airport.'

'Billy Acres?' murmured Chocko thoughtfully. 'Didn't he used to be one of us?'

Mears nodded.

'That's right. Since he left us he's been very useful at keeping us informed about what goes on in the security services. Helps us to keep one move ahead. Like in this case. He picked up a whisper from his colleagues in the police. So, the next move is to get you three and some more of the boys off to London, primed and ready and nearer the action for when we've got more information. You're to go to the barracks at Regent's Park and await instructions.'

Mears looked at his watch.

'Right,' he said. 'Briefing over. Get ready to move out.'

Me, Chris and Chocko were sorting through our kit when Noodle appeared. He was another trooper with our squad, a small but very wiry man. And when I say 'small', I mean small. He was about 5 feet 4 tall, and we used to joke he'd have made a good jockey. Noodle said his height didn't worry him; it meant he had more chance of getting out of small places than bigger blokes. And he was right.

'What's the panic?' he asked. 'I was just settling down to a bit of leave at home,

18

when my bleeper went, and the Duty Officer told me to join you three erks here.'

'Something's going on at the Ajanian Embassy,' Chocko told him.

'What?' asked Noodle.

We all shrugged.

'It's got to do with hostages,' said Chocko. 'Otherwise they wouldn't be sending for us. I mean, if it was a shooting it'd be all over the news by now and we'd know about it. If it was a bomb, then the bomb-disposal squad would've been called in. Stands to reason, there's got to be hostages involved.'

'Listen to Sherlock Holmes!' chuckled Chris.

'It must be all that chocolate he eats,' said Noodle. 'Makes his brain work better.'

'OK, Sherlock,' I said, 'if it's hostages, who's holding 'em?'

Chocko thought for a second, then replied: 'Someone from the embassy. One of the staff. He's taken hostages because he wants to get political asylum here.'

I shook my head.

'In that case, he wouldn't do it in the Ajanian Embassy,' I reasoned. 'No, if there are hostages involved, it'll be someone from another country who's gone into the Ajanian Embassy.'

'Why?' asked Chris.

'Who knows,' said Noodle. 'Anyway, we won't find out standing here. Let's get this stuff loaded up and on our way.'

We double-checked our equipment packed in the back of the lorry. Although it was supposed to be in order already, we're great believers in double-checking. You get that way when your life depends on your equipment.

Weapons: Heckler and Kock MP5 sub-machine-guns. This was a change of weapon for us. Up till now we'd usually used the Ingram sub-machine-gun, and before that the Sterling sub-machine-gun. In my opinion the Heckler and Kock seemed to be an improvement on them – German weapons engineering at its best.

Then the rest of our weaponry: Browning high-power handguns. Remington pump-action shotguns; very useful if you have to open a door the quick way, by blowing away the locks and hinges. Browning 9mm pistols, which we sometimes used as a back-up weapon. Flash-bangs (stun-grenades).

Then there were our explosives. Regular explosives used for blowing open doors. Also the clacker – a little dynamo that produces enough electricity to blow a charge when you pressed its small handle. We checked the boxes containing our clothing: black overalls, belt kit, lightweight boots, body armour, respirator, gloves, assault waistcoat loaded with flash-bangs. Finally, ropes for abseiling, night goggles, helmets, sledge-hammers.

'All present and correct,' said Chris.

'Right,' said Noodle. 'Off we go.'

We signalled to the lorry driver that we were ready.

'Follow us,' Chocko told him. 'But if we get separated for any reason, head for the barracks at Regent's Park in London. We'll RV there. OK?' By 'RV' he meant rendezvous.

The driver nodded and got into the lorry. We four headed for the Range Rover.

'Who's driving?' asked Chris.

'Dave,' said Noodle. 'He needs the practice. He's got to be the worst driver I've ever been with.'

'Cheek,' I said. 'I'm as good as you any day.'

'Oh yeah?' said Noodle. 'Who was it who reversed through a shop window in Beirut?'

'Someone was firing a missile at us,' I reminded him. 'I had to take evasive action, if you remember.'

'With luck, no one will be firing missiles at you today,' said Chocko. 'Come on, Dave, you're nominated. Get behind the wheel.'

Chapter 3
HOSTAGE SITUATION

We arrived at Regent's Park Barracks at 21.30. After parking the Range Rover, we walked into the main building. There we met another bloke from our squad, Mucker Johnson, who grinned and looked pointedly at his watch.

'You've taken your time, haven't you?' he said. 'We've been here for hours.'

'Some of us have come all the way from Hereford,' retorted Chris. 'Some of us keep training twenty-four hours a day, seven days a week. We don't have time to swan around London, living a life of leisure.'

Mucker chuckled.

'Some of you need extra training,' he said. 'Anyway, come on in. The briefing's in the hall.'

As we walked along the corridor with Mucker, I asked him: 'What's the score?'

'Terrorists have taken over the Ajanian Embassy,' said Mucker. 'They've got hostages and are threatening to shoot them.'

'See,' said Chocko, smugly. 'I told you.'

'What sort of terrorists?' I asked. 'Where are they from?'

Mucker shook his head. 'Not sure,' he said. 'I suppose that's what we're here to find out.'

By now we were at the hall. We walked in and saw that the top brass had really pulled out all the stops on this one. There were about forty SAS blokes there. This was obviously going to be a really big job. We had barely time to get through the door before a voice called out, 'Gentlemen, take your seats.'

As we sat down, the top SAS man in the country – or the Director of the SAS, to give him his official title – Brigadier Peter Armstrong, or the Brig, walked in from a side door. With him was our commanding officer, Lieutenant-Colonel Webster.

'Gentlemen,' said the Brig, 'most of you will know by now that we have a hostage situation in the Ajanian Embassy at Hyde Park. At the moment, police negotiators are trying to talk the terrorists into letting the hostages go and giving themselves up.'

The Brig looked towards the door and called, 'Lights!' The lights went down and we began to watch a slide show. The first slide was of the Ajanian Embassy itself, a large old-fashioned, white-fronted building.

'The Ajanian Embassy,' announced the Brig. 'At sixteen Prince's Gate. From what we can gather, at 11.25 hours this morning some terrorists entered it, producing guns as they did so. We don't know how many terrorists there are, nor how many hostages they've taken. We also don't know the details of the terrorists' weapons, but we know they work. Shots were fired.

'As they went into the embassy, they took the policeman on duty outside with them at gunpoint. PC Jimmy Preston is a member of the Diplomatic Protection Group. He attempted to resist, but he was overpowered.

'When they began firing, some of the people inside the embassy tried to get out through the rear windows. Two were lucky and did indeed get to safety this way, as did another man who got out through a first-floor window and managed to get to an adjoining building. They are helping us now with information about what's going on inside the embassy.

'The Ajanian *Chargé d'Affaires*, Dr Ahmed Aziz, also tried to escape, but he wasn't so lucky. He jumped from a first-floor window. He was injured when he landed and the terrorists dragged him back inside the embassy. We don't know how serious his injuries are. However, that means we have at least one injured hostage inside.

'As well as embassy people, the other hostages include a BBC producer and sound-recordist, Paul Wilson and Andrew Duffield, who were getting visas to visit Ajan. As I've already said, we don't know exactly how many hostages are being held, apart from PC Preston and the two BBC men.'

'The police have reacted very swiftly. Special units have sealed off the entire area. Police marksmen, anti-terrorist officers and officers from the Special Patrol Group are all in place, along with Scotland Yard's Technical Support Branch.'

The slide showing the Ajanian Embassy disappeared and was replaced with one of a similar building.

'This is number fifteen Prince's Gate, the building next to the embassy. The police have taken it over as a temporary base. From here they have been able to establish a field-telephone link with the terrorists through a window. Outside telephone communications to the embassy have been cut off.

'Already, an interpreter has been brought in to work with the police at number fifteen. There is also a psychiatrist there who has experience of siege situations.

'So far, the terrorists have told the police negotiator that they are members of DRFLG, the Democratic Revolutionary Front for the Liberation of Gunistan. Gunistan is a small oil-rich province of Ajan whose people are mainly ethnic Arabs. A bit of history for you, gentlemen. Gunistan was invaded and taken over by Ajan in 1926. According to our intelligence reports, the mainly Arab population of Gunistan has been persecuted by their ethnically Persian Ajani rulers. More worrying, as far as our intelligence services are concerned, is that DRFLG is backed by the neighbouring country of Pazia. Pazia, as you know, has been a sore point with us for some time.

'The DRFLG terrorists have issued some demands. They want the release of ninety-one Gunistanians held in prisons in Ajan. They also demand safe passage for themselves out of England. If these demands are not met by 18.00 tomorrow, the hostages will be killed.'

The Brig let this sink in, before he added firmly. 'It is not the policy of Her Majesty's Government to give in to the demands of terrorists. This afternoon I attended a meeting of a Cabinet committee where I was told that the terrorists will not be allowed to leave the country. The police are to negotiate for as long as it takes to achieve a peaceful outcome. However, the Government has decided that if two of the hostages are killed, then there will be an assault on the embassy to rescue the remaining hostages and to terminate the terrorists. And that is where you come in.

'You will be split into two teams, Red

Team and Blue Team. Red Team will stand by for Immediate Action, or IA. Meanwhile Blue Team will begin preparing a Deliberate Assault Plan, or DAP. The two teams will swap roles every twelve hours.'

Chris and I looked at one another and nodded approvingly at this. Immediate action would mean exactly that: going into the embassy with no planning, using sledge-hammers to open ground-floor doors, at the same time as breaking in through the upper windows, and clearing the place room by room with CS gas. It was our least preferred option. It would only be used if the situation deteriorated so much that there was no time for a DAP.

A DAP was our favoured course of action because we would be in control. Or, at least, as much as anyone can be in control in a hostage situation. A DAP is launched when the SAS think the time is right – for example, when the terrorists are exhausted and the exact location of the hostages is known. The reason for swapping every twelve hours is because it's difficult to maintain the edge needed for IA for longer than twelve hours.

'Right, gentlemen,' the Brig finished. 'We

hope that the siege will be over soon. However, if it isn't, then that's when you come in, and the lives of those hostages will be in your hands.'

Chapter 4
PLAN OF ACTION

The deadline was set for 18.00 hours. I looked at my watch. 00.45 hours. That meant the police negotiators had just over seventeen hours to get this situation sorted out peacefully. If they didn't and people started being killed, we'd be called in. Providing the terrorists were telling the truth, of course. For all we knew they may have already killed one or more of the hostages. So far, apart from the fact that some DRFLG members were holding hostages and threatening to kill them unless their pals in Ajan were released, no one knew much.

Me, Chris, Chocko and Noodle and about sixteen other blokes were assigned to Red Team. We had been given the Immediate Action strategy and so if things suddenly started to go wrong, we'd be straight in.

31

At 01.00, fully kitted up, we clambered into a large furniture-removal lorry with armour-plated sides and rumbled through the streets towards Prince's Gate. As we neared the Ajanian Embassy, we could see TV cameras and lights through the windscreen. It was like a film set.

'Great!' groaned Noodle. 'We're gonna be on telly. If the terrorists have got a TV set in there, they'll know exactly what's going on.'

Our removal lorry turned into a small side-street at the end of Prince's Gate. We waited for a bit, hearing the sound of metal being dragged along outside. Then the back doors were opened and a policeman, wearing body armour over his uniform, gestured to us.

'OK, everybody out,' he said. 'No hanging about. Straight up those steps.'

We came out of the lorry fast, as we always do, but there was no danger of being caught on camera. Screens had been dragged across the side street, blocking the view from the waiting TV cameras. This was important to us. When you're in the SAS you can become a target for all sorts of terrorists, so the last thing you want is your face being splashed all over the media.

We ran up the steps and in through the side-door of a large building. I spotted a brass plate on the wall, which read: Royal College of General Practitioners.

'We're in the top doctors' HQ, lads,' I said.

'Let's hope we don't need them,' quipped Chris.

As we headed downstairs to our control room in the basement, we saw that there was a buzz of activity inside the building – people in different uniforms running up and down stairs, in and out of rooms carrying clipboards, talking and listening to radio-telephones, all with serious expressions on their faces.

The basement room had everything we needed: tables and chairs, two settees, a TV set, a sink, electric kettle, cups and plates. Magazines were also lying on the tables. Not only medical ones, but others on cars, boats and interior decorating. Plenty to read, and plenty of space to relax in. It would make a change for us to be waiting in a nice warm room in cosy chairs with all the comforts of home. Usually on a mission, we'd be lying in mud, or up to our necks in stinking swamp water, swallowing huge tropical bugs and insects every time we opened our mouths.

We all made for the easy chairs and settled down. We knew from experience that this situation could go one of two ways: either it would be over in a very short time, or it could be a very long wait. If the latter, it was good to have somewhere pleasant to while away the time.

We'd barely sat down before one of our commanding officers, Colonel Jackson, walked in.

'OK, lads,' he announced. 'First, to let you know where you are. This is going to be our FHA, our Forward Holding Area. This is number fifteen Prince's Gate, the home of the Royal College of General Practitioners, who have kindly loaned it to us for the duration of this situation.'

'Like they had a choice,' whispered Chris to me out of the corner of his mouth, grinning as he did so.

'Next door is our target, the Ajanian Embassy,' continued Jackson. 'We also have access to other buildings in this street, notably the Nubian Embassy at number twenty-four, which is right across from the Ajanian Embassy. Again, everyone is being very co-operative. Everyone except the terrorists, that is.

'You're the IA squad at the moment. So, stand by. If anything happens, you know what to do: you go in.'

He looked at his watch.

'It's now zero three hundred. I'll update you with further briefings as and when we hear anything.'

With that, Jackson left the basement room, and the chatter started up among us.

'Anyone fancy a game of cards?' called out Terry. 'If we're going to be stuck here, might as well put it to profitable use.'

Terry was the squad's gambler. Cards. Horses. Football. Terry would put a bet on almost anything. It wasn't as if he won, either. Most of the time he seemed to lose. But then, Terry didn't seem to care about winning or losing money, it was gambling itself that fascinated him. If he saw two drops of water running down a window-pane he'd say, 'Anyone fancy betting which one gets to the bottom first?'

'Don't tell me you've bought a pack of cards with you!' laughed someone else.

Terry grinned.

'Of course,' he said, producing a small dog-eared pack from inside his outfit. 'You never know when they'll come in useful.'

While some of the guys pulled their chairs round a table for a game and Terry started to shuffle the cards, Chris, Chocko, Noodle and I made ourselves comfortable. We talked tactics: who'd be the one using the sledge-hammer if the call came for us to go in.

'Well, it's got to be me,' said Chocko. 'I mean, I'm the strongest. I've got the biggest arms.'

'Oh, come on!' laughed Chris. 'Just because you've got the biggest arms doesn't mean they're the strongest. If you ask me, most of that's fat.'

'Fat!' said Chocko, indignantly.

'Chris has got a point,' put in Noodle. 'I mean, you can't eat as much chocolate as you do and not get fat.'

'They're like concrete,' said Chocko, annoyed. 'I can crack nuts in the crook of my arms.'

'You're too mean to buy a proper nut-cracker?' I chuckled.

Chocko was not to be joked out of his indignation.

'I can prove my arm muscles are stronger than any of yours,' he said. 'I'll arm-wrestle any one of you.'

'It's a bet,' said Noodle. 'How much for? Fiver? Tenner?'

'Give over, Noodle,' said Chris. 'Even if Chocko's arms are all fat, he's so much bigger than you you'd be throwing your money away.'

'My arms are not fat!' repeated Chocko.

For a moment I thought Chocko was going to get really upset and have a go at Chris, but just then there was a call from the door: 'OK, lads! Let's have your attention!'

We all looked up as Sergeant Moffat came in. With him was one of the senior police officers in charge of the operation, carrying a folded sheet of paper.

'Men, this is Chief Superintendent Oxley,' announced Moffat. 'He's got some info to share with you, so sit up and take notice.'

'Thank you, Sergeant,' nodded Oxley.

'We've managed to track down the caretaker from the embassy. Luckily for him, yesterday was his day off, so he didn't get caught by the terrorists. In fact, he didn't know anything about the siege until he heard it on the news this morning, just as he was setting off to work. From him we've been able to get up-to-date information about the layout of the embassy. We've passed this on to your senior officers. I understand they are making arrangements to recreate the interior of the embassy so that you can familiarize yourself with it, in case you need to go in.'

They'd be recreating it inside the Killing House at Hereford, I thought. Making it look as real as possible.

Chief Superintendent Oxley unfolded his sheet of paper.

'Right,' he told us. 'The caretaker says the building has six floors, including the basement, and fifty rooms. The ground- and first-floor windows have toughened glass and the front door is armour-plated.'

Chocko, Noodle, Chris and I exchanged looks. Good to know that. Sledge-hammers would have bounced off the door – perhaps even off the windows too – leaving us standing out on the pavement like idiots.

'In other words,' added Sergeant Moffat, 'going in through the ground floor or the first floor is out, unless we blow the windows. Plus there's another piece of information that might interest you. The terrorists have made contact with the police negotiator. They have told him that they've wired the embassy with explosives. If there is any attempt to storm it, they'll set them off ... So, gentlemen, start thinking. How do we get in without killing everybody?'

Chapter 5
PLANE COVER

After Sergeant Moffat and Chief Superintendent Oxley had gone, all of us in Red Team looked at one another. We were all thinking the same thing. If Immediate Action was called for, how did we get in?

'The roof,' said Terry. 'Down through a skylight, if there is one.'

'Say they've wired it?' asked Donny.

Donny was one of our best men on explosives. It was well known that he could make a small bomb out of almost anything, which meant that he was always thinking: if I can do that, so can someone else. This made him a great man to have on your team, always thinking ahead to where there might be a booby-trap of explosives.

'That's our biggest problem,' said

40

Noodle. 'No information. We don't know how many of these terrorists there are. It could be just one bloke and a handgun making fools of us all.'

'People who tried to escape were dragged back inside. That means more than one person,' Chris pointed out.

'So how many? Two? Three? A dozen?' asked Chocko. 'We don't even know how many hostages are being held.'

'So, we find out,' I put in. 'Microphones in the walls. Cameras if we can get them.'

'I think MI5 have already set up the cameras,' said Jacky. 'I spotted some in the building opposite. Telephoto-lens stuff.'

'Yeah, but there's no sign of mikes,' I said again. 'Let's put some in, then we can find out what they're talking about.'

'Good thinking,' nodded Chocko. 'OK, that's you and me on drilling duty, Dave. Right?'

'Sounds good to me,' I agreed.

While Chocko went to fetch the drills, I went up to the first floor and listened at the party-wall. You have to be careful when planting a hidden microphone in a wall. You have to drill a hole for the microphone to go in, getting it as near as you can to the wallpaper of the building on the other side of the wall. If you don't drill the hole deep enough, the sound is muffled. If you drill too far and go through the wallpaper, you've blown it. It's a very slow job as well, because you can't use an electric drill: the sound would alert the people in the other building that something was happening. So you have to use one of those old-fashioned drills with a handle that you turn. Like I said, very slow, and also very nerve-racking, because you're worried in case you drill too far.

Chocko arrived with the drills and I set to work in a room on the ground floor, while Chocko started on the first floor. I drilled slowly into the brickwork behind the plaster of the wall, trying to keep noise to an absolute minimum. It was such slow work that it felt like it was going to take days to drill a hole deep enough to push a single microphone into the wall. Suddenly there was a sharp tap on my shoulder. A policeman pointed at the drill, shook his head and drew a finger across his throat. Cut it. Stop the drilling.

I pulled out the drill and we went into

the corridor so that we were away from the party-wall.

'What's the problem?' I asked.

'The terrorists have been on the phone. They can hear noises from the wall. They're worried that we're trying something and they're threatening to kill the hostages now if it goes on.' He gestured at the drill I was holding. 'It's you and your mate, drilling.'

I let out a groan.

'How can they hear us?' I demanded, annoyed. 'I'm drilling so slowly you'd need ears like a bat to be able to hear it from there. Can't you tell them it's mice?'

'Mice?' echoed the policeman, in disbelief.

'Yes. Mice in the walls. There's bound to be some in these old buildings.'

The policeman shook his head and looked at me as if I were an idiot.

'You don't expect they'd believe that, do you?' he said.

'Well, we've got to try something,' I insisted. 'We've got to get these microphones into the wall so we can find out what they're up to.'

Then an idea struck me – this one even more outrageous than trying to fool the terrorists with noisy mice in the walls. It was so outrageous, it made me smile.

'What's so funny?' asked the policeman.

'I'll tell you later,' I said.

With that, I hurried down to the basement room.

There, Colonel Jackson was studying architect's plans of the Ajanian Embassy on a table in front of him.

'Excuse me, sir,' I said. 'We've got a problem with planting these microphones. The terrorists can hear us, no matter how slowly we drill. We need to get these microphones in today, not next week. We need some noise to cover the drilling.'

Jackson could obviously tell that I had an idea from the grin on my face.

'You're not planning to blow things up outside the front door, I hope,' he said.

'No, sir,' I said. 'But how about getting some workmen to mend a burst pipe or something? They'd have to dig up the road, wouldn't they? The noise they'd make should cover our drilling.'

Jackson thought about this briefly, then nodded.

'Good idea,' he said. 'I'll get on to it straight away.'

He picked up the red phone on the table and started to dial. As he did so, I tried out my really outrageous idea on him.

'And planes, sir,' I said.

Jackson looked puzzled.

'Planes?'

'Yes, sir,' I nodded. 'If the planes going in and out of Heathrow could fly a little lower ...'

Jackson laughed.

'Using jumbos to cover the noise,' he chuckled. 'I like that! Right, I'd better pass that on to the commander. Getting the gas board to dig up a street, I think I can manage. Getting planes to fly lower will need someone with more gold on his uniform than I've got.'

I went back upstairs, congratulating myself on my good idea. As I reached the top of the stairs, I ran into Chocko.

'What are you looking so pleased with yourself for?' he demanded. 'I've just had some idiot copper telling me to stop drilling.'

'That's just what I've been sorting out, Chocko old lad,' I told him. 'I've just been re-routing Heathrow's planes. No problem!'

And as it turned out, it wasn't. Thirty

minutes later, Colonel Jackson called me down to the basement.

'You've got what you wanted, Harris,' he said. 'The gas board are on their way to start tearing up the road just a street away – a "gas leak" that needs to be dealt with urgently. Shortly, there'll be a report on the news about it and the traffic chaos it'll cause in central London, so that'll hopefully set the terrorists' minds at rest. As for the planes, air-traffic control will start bringing them lower as soon as they can. They'll phone to tell us when one's coming over flying particularly low. You'll have to work as fast as you can once all that covering noise starts.'

And we did. When the gas board crew turned up and started tearing up the road, Chocko, Chris and I set to work with a vengeance. Whenever we had the additional cover of a low-flying passenger jet, we allowed ourselves to drill a little harder and faster. The noise and vibrations caused by a low-flying jumbo were incredible. It made me glad I didn't live right beneath a Heathrow flight path. I would have had a permanent headache.

We'd managed to get six holes drilled,

when Sergeant Moffat arrived and informed us that it was nearly 15.00 hours and time for a change-over. Blue Team were going on to IA. We were being taken back to Regent's Park Barracks.

There were only three hours to the terrorists' deadline of 18.00 hours.

back to barracks.

The...

Chapter 6
HOSTAGE RELEASE

The journey in the removal lorry back to
the barracks was a lot slower in daytime.
Even with our police escort, the traffic kept
us at a snail's pace. To pass the time, we
listened to the news on the radio. It didn't
sound good. The terrorists' demands for
the Ajanian Government to set their pals
free had been turned down flat. In the
weird world of international politics, where
politicians of all nations are suspicious of
every other politician, the Ajanians seemed
to think this whole siege business was a
trick by the Americans. We heard a
spokesman from the Ajanian Government
tell an interviewer: 'These so-called
terrorists are actually CIA agents. The
Americans have engineered this invasion
of our embassy in London as a way to
pressure the Government of Ajan into

releasing the Americans that are being held in Ajan.'

The Americans he was referring to were diplomats who had been caught in Ajan when the Shah of Ajan had been overthrown by a revolution about a year ago. They'd been taken hostage by the new Ajanian Government and been held prisoners ever since. Earlier in the year, the Americans had sent in their special forces to rescue their diplomats. It had been a military disaster. The special forces had taken casualties and had been forced to abandon the mission.

Back then Chris had remarked to me that 'They should have sent us in. We'd have got them out.' I wondered if he'd be so confident now. It looked as if we were going to have a hard enough time rescuing our own hostages in the centre of London, let alone rescuing hostages from deep inside Ajan.

On the radio, the man from the Ajanian Government then made an even more chilling statement: 'The hostages should consider it an honour to die as martyrs for the revolution.'

'Oh yeah?' said Noodle sarcastically. 'It's

all right for him to say that. He's not sitting inside that embassy with someone poking a gun in his ear.'

'And I'm not sure those two BBC blokes will be happy to be martyrs, either,' put in Chocko.

We arrived at the barracks and headed for our bunks. But none of us could sleep, not with the clock ticking down towards the deadline. It was 16.30 hours. Only ninety minutes to go. I couldn't help myself watching the minutes go by. The deadline came ever nearer, second by second. And then it was here, 18.00 hours. I could sense the tension in the room. All of us waiting for something to happen. But nothing did. The deadline came and went. There were no reports of any of the hostages being killed.

I waited until the clock showed 18.30, then I said to Chris, 'That's it. The deadline's passed and nothing's happened. I'm putting my head down for an hour or so. If there's any action, wake me up.'

'Don't worry,' grinned Chris. 'If anything happens, you can be sure we'll all be woken up soon enough.'

*

I woke up three hours later and was told that there were no reports of any shooting. As far as we knew, the hostages were still alive and negotiations with the terrorists were continuing. So far so good, I thought.

'That doesn't mean that the terrorists haven't done something,' pointed out Chocko, as we sat in the mess grabbing some food. 'They could have killed a hostage or two and not told anyone.'

'But the point about killing a hostage is to show you mean business. You don't keep it secret,' said Chris.

Just then the music on the radio stopped and a voice said, 'We interrupt this programme for a news bulletin about the siege at the Ajanian Embassy in London.'

This is it, I thought. They've killed one of the hostages. We're going in.

We were all on our feet and moving towards the door, when the announcer continued, 'One of the hostages, Paul Wilson, a BBC producer, has been released due to illness. More details will follow as we receive them.'

And then the music started again.

Immediately we all started talking. Not a hostage killed, but one released. One of the

51

British hostages. Due to illness, they said. What sort of illness? The sooner we could talk to this Paul Wilson and find out what was really going on inside the embassy, the better.

Within thirty minutes, an ambulance came in through the main gate of the barracks. Ten minutes later we were gathered round Paul Wilson. He looked ill all right, there was no denying that. He lay on a bed, his head propped up on a pile of pillows, looking pale and haggard, sweat gleaming on his face.

'What's he got?' I whispered to the guy next to me, a small Scot nicknamed Wee Tam.

'Some tropical disease, I hear,' Wee Tam whispered back. 'Apparently he caught it when he was out in Africa.'

'How come he's caught it again?' I asked, puzzled.

'Stress,' said Wee Tam knowledgeably. 'It can bring it back.'

Meanwhile, our guys were starting to fire questions at the sick man. How many terrorists are there? What sort of weapons have they got? Is the building wired to blow up? How many hostages?

'Gentlemen!' said a tall man, holding up his hand to quieten the questions. 'I am the doctor in charge. It was only because Mr Wilson insisted that I reluctantly agreed to let him talk to you – or be debriefed, as I believe you call it – before he goes to hospital. Mr Wilson is very ill. Therefore, I would ask that you don't all shout at him at once. Please, let him speak first, then you can ask your questions.'

We all fell silent. Wilson, despite his suffering, forced himself to speak.

'There are six of them,' he said. 'They are all armed. The leader calls himself Salim. He seems to be calm, but the others are very excitable. Very jumpy.'

'Are the doors and windows wired with explosives?' I asked.

Wilson shook his head.

'I don't think so,' he said. 'They didn't appear to have explosives. Just guns and grenades. But they could have fixed grenades to some of the windows, I suppose.'

'How many hostages are there?'

'Twenty-six. Eighteen members of staff, including six women, plus eight visitors. So now there are twenty-five left.'

'What's the condition of the man who was injured?' I asked. 'The Ajanian *Chargé d'Affaires*?'

'Dr Ahmed Aziz,' nodded Wilson. 'He sprained his ankle, but apart from that he's comfortable. He insists on staying inside the embassy with the other hostages.'

'What sort of weapons have they got?' asked Chris.

Wilson shook his head.

'I'm sorry,' he said. 'I don't know the difference between types of guns. All I know is they've got some machine-guns and some pistols.'

There was an awkward silence at this answer. Frankly, this wasn't much help to us. We needed details. Then Noodle spoke up.

'Would it be OK if we showed Mr Wilson some guns?' he asked the doctor. 'And some pictures of guns. He might be able to recognize the kinds he saw.'

The doctor looked at Wilson, who nodded.

'I'll do my best,' he said.

There was a great rush as we all went to grab our weapons, but once again the doctor spoke up.

'I must stress that my patient has been under a great deal of strain –' he began.

Sergeant Moffat interrupted the doctor, speaking quietly, but very deliberately.

'If we don't find out everything we can about how these men are armed, the rest of the hostages may find themselves under even more strain, doctor. They could end up dead if we get it wrong.'

His softly spoken words had the impact required and the doctor nodded.

'I understand. Go ahead,' he said.

As quickly as we could, and with concern for the sick man holding our impatience in check, we showed Wilson our weapons and pictures of guns and grenades.

After fifteen minutes, when it was obvious that he was struggling to stay awake, we had as much information as we could get from him.

As the ambulance men carried Wilson out, we took stock of what he had told us.

If Wilson's identification had been correct – and we had to allow for the fact that he was unfamiliar with guns and also very ill – the six terrorists were armed with two Polish Skorpion W263 sub-machine guns, three Browning self-loading pistols, one 0.38 Astra revolver and five Russian RGD-5 hand-grenades. It was a formidable arsenal. If we had to go in, we were going to have one serious fight on our hands.

Chapter 7
DELIBERATE ASSAULT PLAN

After Wilson had been taken away, Sergeant Moffat told us to go to one of the large halls at the back of the barracks. As we walked into the hall, an amazing sight met our eyes. Sheets of brown hessian sacking hung from rails across the ceiling, looking like a maze. Then I realized what we were looking at.

'It's the inside of the embassy,' I said.

'Correct,' nodded Sergeant Moffat. 'The lads didn't have time to make it out of wood, like at Hereford, but I think you'll agree they've done a good job. Every room in the embassy has been recreated, to the exact dimensions of the architect's plans. Every door-frame has been left as an opening in the hessian, every window has been cut out where it should be.'

We stared, impressed.

'Incredible!' said Chris. 'Who did it?'

'The Irish Guards,' said Sergeant Moffat. 'Good, eh? I told 'em it was so good they ought to take up needlework. They didn't take it as a compliment.'

Now we had as much information as we could gather, we set to work to refine what Blue Team had already planned for the DAP, the Deliberate Assault Plan.

Blue Team had reached the same conclusion as us: some of the men would go in through the skylights on the roof; the rest would abseil down to the front balconies on the first and second floors and blow out the windows. We all knew that we would have only seconds to enter the building. As soon as the terrorists realized what was going on, they would probably start shooting the hostages. The only way to get it right was to practise the entry over and over again.

We were just starting to practise, when Colonel Jackson arrived. He had the latest demand from Salim and the terrorists.

'Salim wants a bus,' Colonel Jackson told us. 'When he receives news that his friends back in Ajan have been freed, he wants it to take him, his men and all the hostages to an airport.'

'The Government isn't going to go along with that, surely!' snorted Wee Tam. 'Letting them go?'

'Of course not,' said Jackson. 'Our plan is to persuade Salim that the Ajanians have released the prisoners and get everyone on that bus. Once they're on it, we hit them. It's up to you to work out how to do it with minimum risk to the hostages.'

The terrorist's demand for a bus could turn out to our advantage; without knowing it, they could well have played into our hands. So, while half of Red Team carried on training and preparing for the DAP, Chocko, Noodle, Chris, Mucker, Wee Tam, Terry and me set to work on what we called the 'Bus Option'.

The first thing we did was get hold of a forty-seater, single-decker bus. Then we tore it apart to see what we could do with it. One thing soon became clear: there was no room to hide any of us inside it. This meant that the driver had to be one of us.

All of us immediately volunteered to be him, but Noodle shouted us down.

'None of you can be the driver!' he insisted. 'I'm the only one who can do it!'

'Sez who?!' demanded Chris. 'I can drive a bus as well as you! Better, in fact!'

'Driving the bus is nothing to do with it,' said Noodle. 'It's getting out of it that counts.'

Noodle walked to the driver's window.

'The bus drives along until it reaches a prearranged spot, when the driver hits the brakes. Agreed?'

We all nodded.

'As soon as the bus stops, we launch the ambush. Front and rear of the bus, and along one side,' Noodle continued.

Again we all nodded. The reason for hitting it from one side only was because a bus has such thin metal that bullets would go right through it, killing people on the other side.

'As soon as they know it's an ambush, they'll start shooting the hostages,' Noodle carried on.

'No,' said Mucker. 'The first one they'll shoot is the driver, because they'll know he's one of ours.'

Noodle smiled.

'Exactly. So the driver has to get out fast – through the window.'

Noodle tapped the driver's window. Now we understood what he was getting at. The window was about forty-five by twenty centimetres. Noodle was the only person thin enough to get through it. Even then he'd need to be pulled by a couple of blokes outside. We all looked at the grinning Noodle and shrugged, defeated.

'OK,' said Chocko with a scowl. 'You're the driver.'

Pairs of us took turns to drag Noodle through the small bus-driver's window, trying to get it down to the quickest possible time. After we'd done it about forty times, Noodle had bruises down his arms and legs, his ribs, and just about every other part of his body – but it was better to be bruised and escape than to be shot dead. And with me and Chocko pulling him out, we'd got it down to three seconds, from the moment the bus stopped to Noodle hitting the ground outside.

While all this was going on, we kept tuned in to the radio, listening to the news bulletins to pick up as much information as we could about what was going on at the embassy. Things there seemed to be at a stalemate. 'All quiet on the Prince's Gate front,' as Chris put it. But I knew that couldn't last much longer. Hostage situations are dangerously intense. I was certain someone would soon snap under the strain.

Chapter 8
TERRORIST DEMANDS

After grabbing some sleep, we did the change-over: Blue Team returned to the barracks and we went back to the basement, ready for Immediate Action if it was called for.

During our absence the microphones had been installed in the holes between number 15 and the embassy next door.

I decided to go upstairs to check how things were going. One room on the first floor had been set aside as a listening-post. Six people sat at a long desk, each with a headset on, listening to a different microphone. Anything they heard, they wrote down and handed to a uniformed police officer.

This police officer took the handwritten notes to another officer standing beside what looked like a massive plastic game of three-dimensional noughts and crosses. The model had six levels, on each of which were plastic counters, most of them yellow but some of them red. The officer read the notes and moved the counters about.

I stood there, trying to make sense of what was going on. Then it dawned on me: it wasn't a game at all, but a model of the embassy. It was like a doll's house made of clear plastic, with all the interior walls in place, but with the external walls stripped away.

A police officer explained what was happening.

'The people with the headphones are all interpreters,' he said. 'They're listening to conversations, trying to work out who is where in the embassy. If a name is used, then they know who's being talked to, and they can pinpoint where they are. They write that down and pass it on. The officer at the model puts the counter of that person in the correct room. The yellow counters are for the hostages, the red ones for the terrorists.'

'Very impressive,' I murmured. 'It would be useful if we had one of these in the basement so we could keep tabs of where everyone is, just in case we have to go in.'

'Don't worry, you're getting one,' said the police officer. 'It's being made up as we speak. You should have it within a couple of hours.'

I went down to the basement and told the other lads what I'd seen. Everyone was too impatient to wait for our model to arrive, so they wanted to go and see the one upstairs at once. Terry was particularly keen when I told him it looked like a three-dimensional noughts and crosses game. As I've said, he loved playing all types of games.

'Maybe we can keep it after this is over and invent a new game of our own,' he suggested. 'Speaking of games ...'

Terry walked over to the TV set and turned it on. He'd just remembered that the world snooker championships was on. Any thoughts of inventing a new game were immediately forgotten. Most of the other blokes also decided they'd investigate the model house later and settled down to watch the snooker.

Mucker had also been checking things out around the building and he arrived with more news.

'I've just been listening to the conversation between Salim and the police,' he told us. 'It sounds to me like Salim's losing it. He's getting very angry on the phone.'

'I'm not surprised,' said Chris. 'The Pazians have left them in the lurch.'

The gossip from intelligence was that the Pazians had promised to look after the terrorists and to make sure that the British let them go. Now the Pazian Government was keeping quiet. It had got what it wanted out of the situation – stirring up trouble for its old enemy, Ajan. Salim and the other terrorists must have realized that they'd been taken for a ride by the Pazians. They were stuck in London, with no way out of the situation except to give themselves up, or to die.

'Salim's threatening to start killing hostages unless something's done,' continued Mucker.

'Like what?' asked Chris.

'He wants a statement read out on BBC radio news requesting Arab mediators to come in on their behalf.'

'He knows he's got no way out,' I said.

The others nodded in agreement.

Mucker turned to where Terry was watching the snooker.

'Terry, switch channels,' he said. 'See if there's anything on any of the other channels about this. With all those TV cameras out there, there's got to be something.'

'I'm watching the snooker!' Terry protested. 'It's Steve Davis!'

Chocko didn't even bother to argue, he just strode over to the TV set and changed channels.

'I had a bet on that game!' Terry complained.

No one was listening to him. There, live on TV, we could see what was happening on the pavement outside the Ajanian Embassy next door.

A window was open on the ground floor of the embassy. Salim was standing there, holding another man in front of him. He had a gun to the man's head.

Next to them was the policeman who was being held hostage, PC Jimmy Preston. PC Preston was still dressed in uniform – regulation helmet, heavy topcoat buttoned to the collar. He was shouting at the two police negotiators on the

67

pavement. Both of them were wearing bullet-proof vests. We could just about hear what PC Preston was saying.

'Salim wants to talk direct to the media – to the TV and radio people, as well as the newspapers.'

'I'm sorry,' shouted back one of the negotiators, 'that's not possible. But we can give them a statement.'

'I don't want just to give statement!' shouted Salim. 'I don't trust statement! You twist my words if I give statement!'

'No –' began the negotiator, but Salim cut him off. He pushed the gun harder against the head of the man he was holding.

'If I don't talk to media, I kill this man!' he shouted.

'He's gone over the edge,' muttered Chris beside me. 'He's going to do him!'

'Right, lads, looks like we're going in!' shouted Chocko.

I agreed with Chocko. It had been decided that we would go in if two hostages had been killed. But a far as I was concerned, if Salim pressed the trigger, we were go. One dead man almost guaranteed more being killed.

I'd been to many lectures and courses on understanding the psychological aspects of a siege situation, especially the state of mind of the terrorists. One thing was always stressed to us: the point of no return is when a terrorist kills someone deliberately. This is very different from someone being killed by a gun going off accidentally. Before this point there is always a chance for a peaceful resolution. Once this line has been crossed, and someone has been deliberately killed, there is no return for the terrorists. They might as well kill everybody.

We gathered up our guns and ammo and stood, watching the TV screen, waiting for the gun to go off. Instead, the shouting between Salim and PC Preston and the two negotiators continued.

'If he can't talk to the media direct, then Salim wants his statement read out on the radio.'

'In full!' shouted Salim. 'No cutting out bits of my words. Everything I say must be said.'

'Tell him no,' growled Mucker, his sub-machine-gun cradled in his arm. 'Let's go in and get them!'

There was a brief, whispered conversation between the two negotiators, then one of them shouted, 'We'll have to talk to the BBC first and see if they agree.'

'Tell them if they do not agree and my statement is not on the BBC radio news tonight at nine o'clock, I will kill a hostage! If it is read out in full, I shall release one of the hostages.'

With that, Salim and his hostage suddenly disappeared inside. PC Preston hesitated a moment longer at the window, then he too left, shutting the windows as he did so.

The tension in our basement room subsided as we realized that the moment of life and death had passed and everyone was still alive.

'Nine o'clock,' said Chris. 'We've got ourselves another deadline, lads.'

Another deadline. That's the way it goes in siege situations. A deadline is issued to make everyone sit up and take notice. It passes and another one is issued. Then another. And you have to take each and every one seriously. Sometimes it's just part of the mind-game to wear down the opposition. Sometimes a deadline is real. And you never know which it is until it passes. Hope for the best, but expect the worst is what we always say. That's the only way to play it.

The silence was broken by Terry.

'If we're not going in, does anybody mind if I carry on watching the snooker?'

As the time approached 21.00, the whole of Red Team sat in the basement and listened to the radios. We were all fully kitted out: body armour on, guns to hand, gas masks ready to be pulled on when needed. We had two radios turned on: one tuned to Radio 2 and one to Radio 4. I wondered which station Salim and the hostages were listening to.

'The whole statement,' muttered Chris. 'That was what Salim said. The whole statement or a hostage will die.'

'I can't see the BBC doing that,' said Noodle. 'Not a whole statement. I mean, the news is only about a minute or two long. I bet you Salim's demands run to about ten pages. These terrorists always say too much. Words, words, words. They love 'em.'

'Ssh!' snapped Chris.

The pips that signalled 21.00 came from both radios.

We fell silent, and listened.

On Radio 4 there was nothing about the embassy and the terrorists on the first item on the news, nor on the second, nor on the third. My palms were beginning to sweat. Then the newsreader said, 'The terrorists holding the hostages at the Ajanian Embassy in London have issued a demand for Arab mediators to be brought in. Accordingly, the British Government has invited Arab ambassadors to join in the negotiations.'

And that was it. The newsreader started on another story. I didn't even catch what it was about, my only thought was that Salim hadn't got his statement broadcast.

'A couple of sentences, that's all!' called Terry who had been listening to Radio 2.

'Same here,' echoed the Radio 4 listeners.

'Right, that's it!' said Noodle and he headed for the door, all of us following him. Before we could reach it, Sergeant Moffat appeared and realized what was happening.

'Stand down!' he barked.

'But the radio broadcast –' I began.

'The statement went out on the BBC World Service in full,' said Moffat. 'Word for word as Salim wrote it. He's heard it, and he's very happy. He's just told the negotiators so and has agreed to release one of the hostages.' He looked round at us. 'So, they've bought us a bit more time for the moment.'

Chapter 9
SKYLIGHT

The terrorists kept to their word. At 21.30 the front doors of the Ajanian Embassy opened and not one but two people – a woman and a man – came out, their hands held up.

'The police negotiator must've struck a good deal,' said Noodle. 'Two hostages in exchange for a broadcast. We could've done with him on the market stall my uncle used to run.'

As Sergeant Moffat had said, transmitting the broadcast had bought us time, but how much? Ajan were still refusing to let the Arab prisoners go free. Sooner or later Salim and the other terrorists had to realize that their demands weren't going to be met. Once they knew that, they either had to come out and surrender, or carry out their threat to kill the hostages. The whole thing was on a knife-edge and none of us could tell which way it was going to go.

It was back to the waiting game in our basement room. Some of the blokes watched the world snooker on the TV. Some played cards. Me and Chris just sat and waited.

Suddenly Chris whispered to me, 'I'm fed up just sitting around like this. Let's do something.'

'Like what?' I asked.

'It'll be dark outside. What say we go up on the roof, check out the embassy's skylights?'

Chocko had overheard this, and he joined us.

'What if they're wired with grenades, like Salim says?' he pointed out.

Chris looked at me, questioningly.

'What do you think, Dave?'

'Only one way to find out,' I said, and I got up.

Chocko shot a quick glance at the other guys and then muttered, 'Don't think you're keeping me out of this.'

Me, Chris and Chocko took our boots off and put on our trainers. If we were going up on the roof we didn't want to make a lot of noise.

'What are you three up to?' asked Noodle suspiciously.

'We're going for a jog,' said Chocko.

'Like hell you are,' grunted Noodle.

And Noodle also began to take his boots off and put on his trainers. He caught up with us as we were halfway up the second flight of stairs.

'Jogging!' he snorted.

'Jogging on the roof,' grinned Chris. 'We could do with some fresh air.'

The four of us climbed out through the skylight of number 15 and looked along the roof towards the Ajanian Embassy. No one was looking out from their skylights. Although it was dark, there was enough light from the TV cameras and the street lights to see. There's never complete darkness in a city.

'Right,' said Chris. 'Me and Dave take the nearest skylight. You two keep watch. OK?'

Chocko and Noodle nodded. As Chris and I moved carefully across the roof slates towards the skylight, Noodle called after us in a whisper, 'Dave, if you get blown up, can I have your collection of Arsenal football programmes?'

The slates were slippery from lichen growing on them. We moved as quietly as we could, one foot at a time, very slowly, doing our best not to make any noise. We knew that the terrorists would be listening out for the slightest sound. The last thing we wanted to do was make a noise on the roof and startle them into doing something stupid, with tragic consequences.

We reached the embassy's skylight. Slowly and cautiously, Chris edged his head forwards to look down through the glass.

'See anything?' I whispered.

Chris peered more intently.

'It's dark in there, but from the light coming under the door it looks like it's a small bathroom.'

Chris gripped the edge of the skylight and gently pulled at it. I half turned my head away and braced myself against the slates, ready to slide down if it was wired and blew up.

'Drat!' scowled Chris.

I turned to look at him. The skylight was still shut.

'It's bolted on the inside,' he said.

'It could still be our way in if it comes to the crunch,' I said.

Chris nodded.

'Let's open it up,' he said. 'The quiet way.'

I nodded. I knew what he meant. All round the frame of the skylight were strips of lead flashing – edging under the slates to prevent rain coming in. We would have to lift all the lead flashing. Doing it quietly was going to be a long job, but there seemed very little else for us to do that night.

We set to work, sliding the slates out first. Then we used our knives to work loose the nails that held the strips of lead in place. A slow laborious job, but unavoidable. If we had to go in quick, preparing the skylight this way would save valuable seconds. And when you go in, every second saved could be a life saved. Finally, after about half an hour, the last piece of flashing came free.

Chris looked at me.

'One at each end of the frame,' he whispered. 'Lift on the count of three. OK?'

'What if it's booby-trapped?' I asked.

'We won't have to put it back!' grinned Chris.

I took hold of my end of the skylight, working the tips of my fingers underneath the wooden frame. Chris did the same at his end. As we got our grips secure, I reflected that if we'd got it wrong – if the skylight was booby-trapped with explosives and it blew up – it wouldn't just be me and Chris going up. The terrorists would react to what they'd think was an attack and could well start shooting the hostages. For all our sakes, I had to hope that they'd left this skylight untouched, even if they'd booby-trapped and wired the rest of the place.

'OK,' said Chris. 'On three. One. Two. Three.'

We lifted it straight up. There was no explosion.

Chris and I set the skylight down, then peered into the black hole in the roof. As Chris had thought, it was a bathroom. Chris turned the skylight over and released the bolt, and we put the frame back in place.

'This skylight will open now for whoever comes up here next time,' he said. 'We've just made ourselves a way in.'

I was looking forward to doing a bit of

boasting to the rest of Red Team about being up on the roof and opening up a way for our assault, but I never got the chance. When we walked into the basement room it was in semi-darkness and a police briefing was taking place. Chief Superintendent Oxley was standing by a projector and the team were looking at a slide on one of the walls.

Sergeant Moffat growled at us: 'Where have you four been?'

'Jogging, Sarge,' said Noodle, indicating his trainers.

Moffat scowled.

'Jogging, my backside,' he snorted. 'You've been on the roof. If I hadn't been busy down here, I'd have come after you.'

'What's going on, Sarge?' I asked.

'Sit down and you'll find out,' said Moffat.

As we sat down a picture of a man appeared on the wall.

'This is the leader of the terrorists, the one who calls himself Salim,' said Oxley. 'And these are the other terrorists.'

Photos of five other men appeared in turn on the wall. The photos looked like the sort you have taken for a passport. Full face, looking straight ahead. I was stunned at how the police had been able to get hold of them. As Chief Superintendent Oxley started to give details about each of the terrorists, I sidled over to Mucker and asked him, 'How did they get these photos? And the men's names?'

Mucker whispered back, 'Ah, of course, you missed the introduction. That's what you get for trying to be the Lone Ranger.'

'Come on,' I said. 'I'll tell you what we've been up to if you tell me how the police got this information.'

Mucker nodded.

'All right,' he said. 'Ever since this siege started the police have been sending in food and drink and cigarettes.'

'I know,' I said. 'Helps create a feeling of co-operation with the terrorists.'

'It does more than that,' grinned Mucker. 'The food is left on the doorstep in a metal box. Or sometimes it's been handed in through a window, again in a metal box. The box is always handed back for the next lot of stuff.'

A metal box. 'Fingerprints!' I said.

'Exactly,' nodded Mucker with a broad grin. 'You've got to hand it to the police.

Very clever. They've been checking the fingerprints against the hostages to eliminate them. They know the names of all the hostages by now, so the ones who are left are the terrorists.'

'But how did they get these photographs of them?'

'From their passport and visa applications,' said Mucker. 'Like I said, clever, eh?'

Like the rest of Red Team, I committed to memory each of the pictures of the six terrorists. They were the enemy. The hostage-takers. Now I knew the faces of the men I'd be dealing with if it came to it. I knew whom I'd be looking to kill.

Chapter 10
CLOSE TO THE EDGE

Sunday 4 May was the fifth day of the siege. The stalemate continued. The terrorists kept sending out messages repeating their threat to kill the hostages if their demands were not met. The Ajanian Government maintained that they would not release the ninety-one Arab prisoners. The terrorists again asked for Arab ambassadors to be used in the negotiations.

While we were at the Forward Handling Area in number 15, we either watched the snooker on the TV, or played cards, or checked our weapons to make sure there'd be no problems when we went in. Every twelve hours we'd change over with Blue Team and return to Regent's Park Barracks to practise the DAP.

I knew this waiting game was part of

the police's tactics to wear down the terrorists, but, frankly, it was wearing us down as well. We wanted action. That's what we'd been trained for. Yet all we were doing when we were at 15 Prince's Gate was twiddling our thumbs. At least when we were at the barracks we could practise the DAP, using the hessian mock-up.

Sergeant Moffat had assured us that all the mock-up's measurements were accurate and that the doors and corridors inside the embassy were in exactly the same place as they were on the mock-up. The reason this was important was in case the building became so filled with smoke that we couldn't see. In situations like that even a torch is useless, the light just bounces back off the smoke. In the smoke we'd work by touch and by measurement. It's often been a life-saver, knowing that a door is a certain number of paces from the end of a corridor. It can prevent you from blundering into a room unprepared and it can help you to find a way out when there's nothing else to guide you.

We used the hessian mock-up to familiarize ourselves with the embassy, floor by floor, from the top down. A very fancy wide staircase went up the centre of the embassy, with corridors leading off the landings on it. We practised coming in through the big windows at the front and back of the building, then working our way from room to room, along the corridors, always ending up at the staircase. Any hostages we came across would be shepherded to the staircase and sent down it at speed in a file. Any terrorists we came across were to be terminated. No prisoners were to be taken.

Time and again we swung in through the holes in the hessian representing the big windows at the front and back of the embassy to work our way from room to room. As we did so, we counted paces all the time so we'd know where we were. And every time we did it in full kit, so when the time came for the real thing, we'd be able to do it in thick smoke or pitch dark.

That afternoon, Salim released another of the hostages completely unexpectedly. His name was Mohamed Tarkuff and he was a journalist from Syria. He was one of the unlucky visitors who'd been in the Ajanian Embassy when the terrorists had moved in. According to the police, Salim had released him because he was ill with fever. Personally, I had my doubts about this being the real reason. We were at the barracks when they brought Mr Tarkuff in. Although he looked ill, to me it was more like the results of the strain of being kept hostage at gunpoint for five days rather than any real fever. Even so, I was really impressed by him. For a man who'd been held hostage for as long as he had, his mind was very sharp. What he told us about the situation inside the embassy, particularly the relationship between the six terrorists, was really interesting stuff.

'Salim is trying to keep things together, but the other five terrorists are beginning to be unhappy with him as their leader,' he told us. 'They believed Salim when he told them they would all be back home in a day. It has been five days now, and they are wondering what has gone wrong.'

'They can't have expected it to be a walkover?' queried Sergeant Moffat with a frown. 'They're not that gullible, surely?'

'It would appear that they are,' replied

Mr Tarkuff. 'Salim seems to be intelligent and knowledgeable about the world, but the others are all young men from rural areas. I doubt if any of them has been away from home for long before this. None of them appear to be very well educated.'

'So they just thought they'd come here and wave their guns and get what they want?' I said.

Mr Tarkuff nodded.

'It seems that is how things are in their home villages,' he said. 'As I say, they are very naïve young men.'

'Naïve people can be dangerous,' muttered Mucker.

'And these men are dangerous,' said Mr Tarkuff. 'They are unstable.' He sighed. 'Unfortunately, that is also true of some of the members of the embassy staff who are being held hostage. One in particular, a Press Attaché called Abbas. He has taken to arguing with the terrorists.'

'Arguing with them?' echoed Chris. 'Has he got some sort of death-wish?'

'I don't know,' said Mr Tarkuff. 'But the arguments have been very heated.'

'What are they about?' asked Noodle.

'Ayatollah Hassani,' answered Mr

Tarkuff. Ayatollah Hassani was the leader of the Government of Ajan. 'Abbas believes that he can do no wrong. To Abbas, the Ayatollah is the hero of the revolution that overthrew the shah. The younger terrorists have a very different view. They say crude things about him and chant slogans, saying, "Death to Ayatollah Hassani." The situation between the terrorists and Abbas is getting tense.'

'Where does Salim fit in?' I asked.

Mr Tarkuff shook his head.

'He doesn't,' he said. 'He tries to calm everyone down, but the other terrorists are starting to take no notice of him. They are accusing him of betraying them because nothing has happened. Their friends are still in prison in Ajan and they are trapped inside the embassy here in London, and the authorities are refusing to let them leave.'

After Mr Tarkuff had left us and gone to hospital to be checked over, we talked about what he'd told us.

'All that aggression, the frustration, all stuck in the one building. It sounds to me like a disaster just waiting to happen,' said Mucker. 'Lots of edgy fingers on triggers. I've got a feeling one of them is going to be pulling a trigger soon.'

Chapter 11
DEADLINE

The next day, 5th May, the siege entered its
sixth day.

Our top brass obviously felt that things
were about to come to a head at any
moment, because when we went back from
the barracks to 15 Prince's Gate, there was
no change-over with Blue Team. Instead
Blue Team stayed put at the Forward
Holding Area with us. For the first time
since we'd been briefed at the barracks, we
were all together. Word came down to us in
the basement that Salim was on the phone
to the police negotiator. He was demanding
that an Arab ambassador be brought to
the telephone or one of the hostages would
be killed. I decided to nip upstairs to be
near the control room so that I could listen
to the phone conversation.

'I am setting a deadline of half-past one

this afternoon,' came Salim's voice over the speaker connected to the phone. I recognized his voice because I'd heard it before on the speaker and on TV.

'Be reasonable, Salim,' the negotiator said, his voice calm, doing his best to appeal to the terrorist. 'It's impossible to get hold of an Arab ambassador so quickly. But the good news is that the imam at the Regent's Park mosque has offered to come in and mediate. I'm sure you can trust him.'

'That's not enough!' snapped Salim. 'You are not listening to me.'

'I am listening, Salim –' began the negotiator.

But Salim interrupted him and shouted angrily, 'I will kill a hostage unless an Arab ambassador is on this phone by half-past one this afternoon.'

Then the speaker went dead.

I hurried downstairs and told the others what I'd heard.

'It's a bluff,' said Terry. 'We've had deadline after deadline, but has he killed any of the hostages yet?'

'This one could be different,' I said. 'Salim sounded really strung up.'

'Trust me, it's another bluff,' insisted

91

Terry. 'Think about what's happened so far. What's he done to the hostages? He's let them go, one by one. Four of them so far.' He shook his head. 'He's not going to start shooting them now. Not after six days.' He yawned. 'If you ask me, we're wasting our time here. Still, it gives us a chance to watch the snooker championship in comfort.'

Personally, I didn't share Terry's view of the situation. I had heard Salim's voice: it was a voice of a man under stress. And then there was the evidence from Mr Tarkuff. He had impressed me as a man who watched and worked things out. A man who knew where trouble would be coming from. It was the sort of second sense you get when you're a soldier, or a journalist working in war zones. Mr Tarkuff had spent five days in close proximity to the terrorists and if he thought things were going to go bad, things *were* going to be bad. I reckoned we had to be prepared.

I mentioned my opinion to Chris, and he nodded in agreement.

'Let's go up to the control room,' he said. 'See what we can find out.'

*

As the clock ticked away towards the deadline of 13.30, Chris and I went upstairs. We stayed out of the way, not wanting to get ordered back to the basement. As we stood there, the phone rang. The police negotiator picked it up. Then we heard the voice of PC Jimmy Preston over the speaker.

'PC Preston here. I have to warn you that one of the hostages has been tied to the banisters downstairs. They are threatening to shoot him if an Arab ambassador does not come to this phone at once.'

'I'm sorry,' said the negotiator. 'There hasn't been enough time for us to get an ambassador here, but –'

He was interrupted by a voice shouting angrily, 'You are lying!'

It was Salim, beside himself with rage. Either that, or, as Mr Tarkuff had said, he was under pressure to prove to the other terrorists that he could get them out of this, and he thought that shouting at the police would help him.

'Salim, believe me, I am not lying –' began the negotiator in a gentle and concerned tone of voice, but Salim cut him off again.

'The deadline has passed!' he yelled. 'I warned you what would happen if it passed and an ambassador did not speak to us. Let this be a lesson to you! This one is the first to die!'

The room was filled with the sound of a machine-gun being fired, followed by a scream. Then the speaker went dead.

Chapter 12
COBRA

While the police looked at one another, shocked, Chris and I were already hurrying down to the basement.

'They've shot one of the hostages!' Chris announced as we rushed in.

Every man in the room turned to look at us.

'When?' asked Chocko.

'Who?' asked Mucker.

'Looks like we're go at last,' said Noodle, scooping up his gun. 'After all those bruises I got being pulled through that bus window.'

I was leading the way up the stairs, when Sergeant Moffat appeared at the top of them.

'Where do you lot think you're going?' he demanded.

'Taking positions to go in next door,' I said.

'We heard the shots and the scream,' said Chris.

'Not so fast,' said Moffat. 'The politicians aren't so sure someone's been killed.'

'Politicians, hah!' snorted Noodle scornfully. 'I wouldn't trust anything a politician says.'

'Well, in this case you don't have any choice,' said Moffat. 'Until such time as they hand this situation officially over to us, the politicians and the police are still in charge. And they're saying we can't act until we get proof from the terrorists that two of the hostages have been killed.'

'Why two?' demanded Chris.

'In case the first one was killed by mistake. The politicians don't want to send us in if that's what's happened,' said Moffat. 'A second death, accidental or not, is our signal.'

'What sort of proof do they want?' I asked.

'A body,' said Moffat. 'Until then, the politicians think it could be a bluff and they don't want us going in and killing the terrorists if it is. They say it could raise all sorts of awkward diplomatic questions.'

'It could raise even more awkward

questions if they kill one and then go on to kill the rest of them,' said Chocko.

Moffat nodded.

'I agree with you, lad,' he said. 'But right now the chain of command means we can't go in until the operation's handed over to us. So just stand by.'

And so we stood by.

I could see the politicians' point of view – better safe than sorry. However both Chris and I were convinced that the shots and the scream we'd heard had been for real. Someone *had* been killed in the embassy. We both felt that unless something was done soon, more of the hostages would die in the same way. But, all we could do was sit in the basement and wait, and wonder whose screams we'd heard over the loudspeaker.

At 16.30 our top chief, Brigadier Armstrong, arrived. There was a respectful silence as the Brig entered the basement room. He was a big man who'd got to head the SAS by courage, physical prowess and a ruthless intelligence. He was the best of the best. Even Terry turned off the snooker on the telly when the Brig came in.

'Right, men,' he addressed us. 'You all know what happened earlier this afternoon. The terrorists claim to have killed one of the hostages. According to them he was a Press Attaché at the embassy called Abbas.'

Abbas. The same man that Mr Tarkuff had told us about. The man who'd been arguing with the terrorists.

'At the moment we haven't been able to get confirmation that this Mr Abbas has been killed. My own view is that the terrorists have, in fact, carried out their first murder and that we should go in. That's what I've spent this afternoon trying to persuade the politicians to agree to at a meeting of COBRA – or the Cabinet Office in Briefing Room A, to give it its proper title – at Downing Street. However, as you have heard, the politicians want proof that two killings have taken place. I've told COBRA that proof of one killing ought to be enough: we can't play with people's lives here. I've also told them that we've got a better chance of success if we go in before it gets dark. Darkness falls at 20.30 hours, so that gives them less than four hours to make up their minds whether they're going to send us in or not. It's my belief that we could be sent in at any moment. So, I want you all standing by, ready to put the DAP into action as soon as you get the word to go.

'We still have no further information as to whether Salim and the terrorists have wired the building with explosives. I'm afraid, gentlemen, that's a risk you're going to have to take.

'I'm now going back to the COBRA meeting to try to push them off the fence and send us in. If I don't see you before you go in, good luck. And bring the hostages out alive.'

And then the Brig was gone. For us, it was no longer a case of hanging around waiting and getting bored. Chris and I both knew in our hearts that Abbas had been killed in the embassy. It was my guess that the terrorists would show off his body, to let us all know they meant business. Once they did that, we'd be going in. Even though the Brig said the politicians insisted there had to be two killings, I was sure he'd persuade them of the sense of not waiting. If the terrorists decided to kill again, it could turn into a bloodbath inside the embassy.

Chapter 13
SALIM'S THREAT

With Red and Blue Teams combining ideas, we'd worked out the DAP in minute detail. In brief, the plan was as follows.

Red Team would take the top half of the embassy. Half of them would go in through the skylights. The rest would abseil down from the roof to the second-floor balconies. Meantime, half of Blue Team would go in through the first-floor windows and work downwards, clearing the first and ground floors. The rest of Blue Team would go in through the basement and work upwards.

The skylight that Chris and I had already unbolted would be straight-forward. It would just be a matter of opening it and dropping down into the small bathroom. If someone had bolted the skylight shut since our visit, the frame could easily be lifted out. All the nails holding it in place had been taken out by Chris and me; it was only gravity holding the wooden frame in place. The other skylight would have to be blown open with explosives.

While this was going on, me, Chris, Chocko and Noodle would abseil down from the roof to one of the second-floor balconies at the rear of the embassy. Another team of four would abseil down to the balcony next to ours. While we were doing that, Blue Team would be blowing in the windows on one of the first-floor balconies at the front. To do that they'd have to get there from the first-floor balcony at number 15, using a ramp between the balconies. They'd plant an explosive charge against the toughened glass of the window and blow it out.

Meanwhile, the Blue Team members on the ground would blow in the French windows to the basement of the embassy and go in.

If all went to plan, our entry should take just seconds and we'd be in on all the floors at the same time – the top, second, first and the basement, with the ground floor being covered by the teams from the basement and the first floor.

We'd be wearing headsets as well as gas masks. Control would brief us with information from the hidden microphones about where the terrorists were likely to be. Although this plan sounded great in theory, in practice we all knew that we weren't going to be able to hear much over our headsets with explosions going off around the building.

Once we were inside the embassy we'd set off our flash-bangs, our stun-grenades. Then it would be a case of working our way through the rooms. If we found a terrorist, we'd shoot him dead. If we found the hostages, we'd start rushing them down the main staircase to the basement, and out of the back door.

Once the hostages were outside, we'd lay them all face down on the ground, secure their wrists and keep them covered with armed men. This was necessary because you never knew when someone might be a terrorist pretending to be a hostage. For all we knew, one or more of the hostages might even be working with the terrorists. In a life-and-death situation, you can't afford to take chances.

That was the theory. And I knew we

didn't have long to wait to see how it would actually work.

The clock in our basement room ticked round. 16.00 hours. 17.00 hours.

By now we'd read every magazine and every newspaper. The litter bins were filled with rubbish. With only authorized personnel allowed into the building and nothing allowed to be taken out in case it might be needed as evidence later, the rubbish hadn't been collected for the five days we'd been in there. We'd bagged most of it up in black bin bags, which sat in a pile in one corner of the room. It's one of the things we pride ourselves on, clearing up our mess and leaving a place exactly as we found it. It's not just about hygiene, it's about not leaving any traces that might lead to your identity being discovered. In this situation, though, it was simply to avoid living in a tip.

The only one of us who didn't seem to mind the waiting was Terry, who spent most of the time glued to the world snooker championships on the television. The rest of us were starting to get restless, wondering what was going on.

'They could be killing them one by one in there and we'd be none the wiser!' complained Mucker.

'If they were, we'd have heard the sound of shots and they would have been picked up by the hidden microphones,' I pointed out.

We took turns to go up to the listening-post where we were eavesdropping on the embassy through the microphones, but it didn't help much. As the police in the listening-post had promised, we now had our own plastic model of the embassy in the basement, which we updated continuously so that we knew where everyone was. But, for me, at least moving about inside number 15, going up and down stairs, was better than just sitting and waiting in the basement.

Then, at 17.30, word came down to us from the police that Salim had phoned again and demanded that an Arab ambassador arrive at the embassy in the next forty-five minutes, or another hostage would be shot. This hostage's body, together with the body of the one shot earlier, would be thrown out on to the pavement.

'You want proof that we mean business, I will give you proof!' Salim had shouted. 'Two dead bodies. Then another dead body every fifteen minutes until you take us seriously!'

'He's definitely losing it,' Chris said. 'We ought to go in now, before he goes over the edge completely and starts shooting.'

This made us even more impatient. Our job wasn't just to take out the terrorists, it was to try and save the hostages. With Salim making threats in this angry way, we all felt there was a serious risk that a massacre was about to take place inside the embassy.

'What are the police negotiators doing?' burst out Noodle.

'They best they can, by all accounts,' said Chocko, who'd just come into the basement from upstairs, having been listening to the conversation between Salim and the negotiator on the loudspeaker. 'The negotiator's talking to him about the bus, trying to make him think it's all going to be all right.'

'Not the Bus Option again!' snorted Noodle. 'I thought we'd given that one up as a no-hoper.'

'We have,' said Chocko. 'But the negotiator's trying to keep Salim's spirits up. He wants them to think they're going to be getting out of this alive. Maybe that way they won't shoot any more hostages.'

'We still don't know if they actually have shot one already,' said Terry. 'It could have still been a bluff.'

'I think we're about to find out,' said Chris quietly.

We all turned to see what he was looking at on the TV set. The pictures were coming live from Prince's Gate and the camera was homing in on the front door of the Ajanian Embassy. The door was slightly ajar.

'They're opening the door! They're coming out!' said Mucker. 'They're surrendering after all!'

Instead, a limp figure was pushed out and the door slammed shut. The body of a man lay on the steps of the embassy.

'Looks like the politicians have got some of the proof they wanted,' muttered Chris beside me. 'One dead hostage.'

And then we all heard it, echoing down from the loudspeakers upstairs: the sound of more machine-gun fire from

106

inside the embassy. Was this the start of a massacre of all the hostages? One thing was sure: we were go.

Chapter 14
ASSAULT

From that moment, things moved rapidly. The phone rang, and Colonel Jackson took the call. He listened, nodded and said, 'Right, sir', then hung up.

He turned to us and announced, 'That was Lieutenant-Colonel Webster. The Prime Minister's given permission for us to go in.'

'About time!' said Chocko.

'Take your positions,' Jackson told us. 'The signal to go will be "London Bridge" coming through your headsets. As soon as you hear those words, go.'

We gathered up our equipment and filed out of the basement room. Half of Blue Team made for the corridor that headed towards the back of number 15. Their job was to wait under cover, their eyes firmly fixed on the basement entrance to the embassy next door.

We of Red Team moved up the stairs with the rest of Blue Team. Many of Blue Team were weighed down with the explosives they'd need to blow the windows. Others were carrying the ramp for getting to the embassy's balcony.

We, the abseilers of Red Team, carried our ropes. When we got to the first floor, Sammy, one of the leaders of Blue Team, turned and gave me a grin and a thumbs up.

'See you inside the embassy, Dave,' he said.

Then he and the rest of Blue Team headed for the rooms at the front of number 15.

Over the speaker, I could hear the police negotiator on the phone to Salim. The tone of the conversation was chilling, made more so by the relaxed way in which the negotiator responded to Salim's threats, doing his best to calm down the terrorists' leader.

'I will kill all the hostages inside the next five minutes if nothing is done!' Salim raged.

'It is happening, Salim,' said the negotiator. 'An ambassador is on his way here. So there's just the matter of the bus to get sorted out. We've managed to get you a single-decker one, as you requested.'

'Then where is it?!' shrieked Salim. 'There is no sign of this bus!'

'That's what I'm talking to you about right now,' replied the negotiator. 'Where would you like us to park the bus?'

There was a pause, then the negotiator repeated the question, very calmly, 'We are arranging a bus, Salim. Where would you like it parked?'

There was another pause before Salim's voice said, 'Opposite the front door.'

'He thinks they're going to let them get away,' Chris whispered to me.

'Then he's got another thing coming,' I whispered back. 'Once he threw that dead body out on the street, he signed his own death warrant.'

Chris, Chocko, Noodle and I and the rest of Red Team continued on up the stairs, right to the very top. We put on our gas masks and pulled our black balaclavas down over them, fully concealing our faces to prevent our identities from being caught by the TV cameras in the street.

'Test headsets,' came a voice through our earpieces. 'Respond by number.'

One by one we replied through our mikes: Red One, Red Two, Red Three …

Then we climbed the steps to the skylight and hauled ourselves out on to the roof. It was hot out there in the sun. It felt even hotter under our black clothing over body armour back and front, black balaclavas over gas masks, guns, ammo and abseiling equipment.

Me, Chris, Chocko and Noodle moved as quietly as we could towards the back of the embassy. Behind us came the other team of four abseilers for the front. Behind them came Terry and Mucker and the rest of Red Team, heading for the skylights. I attached the end of my rope and made sure it was secure. Chris, Chocko and Noodle joined me. We stood at the edge of the roof, looking down at the rear garden thirty metres below us. I felt a sense of relief. At last, after all the waiting, we were finally going into action and doing what we did best, what we were trained for.

I could see part of Blue Team in the basement area, hidden on the ground, but visible to us from up here. They were crouched behind a low wall, guns ready. Like all of us, they were dressed completely in black, masks covering their faces.

Mucker and Terry had already lifted the skylight that Chris and I had opened earlier, and were standing over the hole in the roof. Two more of Red Team were busy sticking explosives to the second skylight. On the other side of the roof, others were preparing to abseil down the front when the order was given. I wondered how the police negotiator was doing with to Salim.

'Teams, stand by,' said a voice in our headsets.

And then came the words 'London Bridge'. We were go.

Me, Chris, Chocko and Noodle leapt out into space on our ropes, heading for a second-floor balcony below us. At the exact same moment I jumped, I heard an explosion from the roof as the second skylight was blown out. I hit the balcony. Chris and Noodle were next to me.

As they smashed in the windows and threw in the flash-bangs, I looked up to see what had happened to Chocko. His rope had snagged and wrapped itself round his leg and he was dangling just above the balcony. There was no time to help him: our priority was to free the hostages and take out the terrorists before they killed anyone else.

I jumped after Chris and Noodle through the smashed glass into the room. It was empty. The curtains either side of the window had started to smoulder. Then suddenly they burst into flames. The flash-bangs had set them alight.

We didn't have time to put out the flames. Already there was a lot of shouting coming through my headset – orders and questions from Control: where are the hostages? What's your situation? There was too much noise, too much confusion in the mass of radio traffic for us to respond.

Sounds of explosions were coming from the front of the embassy. I guessed Blue Team were blowing their way in through the first-floor windows.

As we pulled open the door of the empty room and burst out on to the landing, smoke from Blue Team's explosions billowed up the staircase.

Through the smoke I saw a door on the

other side of the landing. I knew from the hessian mock-up that this was a small office. The microphones in the walls had picked up sounds from this floor. There could be hostages or terrorists inside that office. There was only one way to find out.

I looked at Chris and gestured at the door. Chris nodded. He took hold of the door handle and pulled the door open, and I ran into the office, gun barrel sweeping from side to side.

There was a man lying on a settee whom I recognized at once from the photos of the terrorists we'd been shown. He was holding a machine-pistol and, as I turned towards him, he raised it straight at me.

Brr-Brr-Brrr!!!!!

I let him have it right across the chest. His body jerked as my bullets hit him. He slumped back on the settee, the machine-pistol falling from his hands to the floor.

One down. Five to go.

Gunfire, explosions, screams and yells filled the embassy. A series of small fires broke out, started by the explosives and the flash-bangs. Quickly, me, Chris and Noodle checked the other rooms on the

114

second floor. They all appeared to be empty. No hostages, no more terrorists.

Chris pointed down to the first floor. Leaving Noodle on guard on the second floor, Chris and I hurried down the staircase to the first-floor landing. The door to a front room was open, so I rushed into it. The room was filled with smoke through which I could see the flicker of flames. Rubble and broken glass was strewn everywhere. Two of Blue Team were picking a man up off the floor. He looked familiar. It was the BBC sound-recordist, Andrew Duffield, covered in dust and debris.

As I watched, the two men from Blue Team pushed him on to the balcony through the remains of the shattered window. Not that there looked to be much balcony left. The guys from Blue Team had obviously used a really big explosive charge because the concrete balustrade had been blown off, hence all the debris in the room. Still, better too much explosive to make sure, rather than too little to get in.

Satisfied that Blue Team had the front of the building under control, Chris and I backed out of the room on to the landing. Here we stood, listening for sounds. Then I heard it, coming from a room to our right: the sound of a struggle, with two men shouting.

I kicked open the door of the room and saw two figures fighting in the centre of the floor. One of them was PC Jimmy Preston. The man he was fighting with was the leader of the terrorists, Salim himself. Salim was holding a pistol and Jimmy Preston was trying to take it off him.

'Jimmy!' I shouted. 'Get away from him!'

But PC Preston was determined that Salim wasn't going to get a chance to kill anyone else: he was set on wrestling the gun off him. My immediate thought was that Salim would shoot Jimmy Preston. As I stood there, the pistol in Salim's hand went off and a bullet ploughed into the carpeted floor. The next one might be into a body.

'PC Preston!' I bellowed. 'Stand down!'

That did the trick. Jimmy Preston released his grip on Salim and pushed himself away from the terrorists' leader. A brave thing to do when you know the other man has a loaded gun. I hoped that Salim would be torn between taking a shot at two targets – me or PC Preston – and that that second's hesitation would give me my chance.

Salim wavered a moment before swinging the pistol round towards me. That was enough. I pressed the trigger of my H & K and let him have three bursts. He was hurled backwards by their force and crashed to the floor. Dead. Two down.

Jimmy Preston stood motionless, looking down at the dead Salim. He was obviously in a state of shock. There was no time to let him stand there. Our plan called for us to get the hostages down the stairs and out of the building as fast as possible. I grabbed him by the shoulder of his greatcoat and hustled him out of the door. As we reached the landing, I saw Chris and Noodle with more of the hostages. They were hurrying them down the stairs to the next floor. I gave PC Preston a shove and he joined the line being shepherded to safety.

Below me, I could see some of Blue Team taking up positions on the stairs so that they could grab the hostages as they passed and push them on to the next guy, keeping up the momentum.

But where were the other four terrorists? I scanned the landing area nervously, expecting one to jump out at any second, aiming a machine-gun at me. Where were they?

Chapter 15
MISSING TERRORIST

While all this was going on inside the embassy, Sammy and Karl from Blue Team crept out on to the first-floor balcony of number 15. Karl was carrying the lightweight ramp. On the 'go' command of 'London Bridge', he dropped the ramp so that it formed a bridge from the balcony of number 15 to the one at the front of the Ajanian Embassy. Close behind Sammy and Karl, in a first-floor room of number 15, were two more of Blue Team, Bunjy and Mick. Bunjy was holding the remote-control for the detonator.

Sammy and Karl rushed across the ramp and fixed the explosives to the embassy's windows. Then they scurried back across the ramp to number 15, Sammy shouting out 'Fire!' as they did so. Bunjy detonated the explosives. The glass in the windows vanished, along with much of the balcony's concrete balustrade. If Sammy and Karl had stayed there, they'd have been blown to bits.

The whole of the front of the embassy was hidden by smoke and dust from the explosion. Sammy and Karl rushed back over the ramp and into the embassy through the shattered windows. Bunjy and Mick followed them. They found a man lying on the floor, covered in plaster from the collapsed ceiling, glass from the window and bits of concrete from the balcony. It was Andrew Duffield, the sound-recordist. They hauled him to his feet and pushed him out on to the balcony for safety. It had been at that point that I'd come into the room, seen them at work, and left them to it.

Afterwards, Sammy and Karl started checking the rest of the rooms on the first floor. In the second one they came to, they found six hostages lying on the floor, guarded by two armed men. Another hostage, a man, was near by, shot dead. Next to him was a man who'd been shot in the legs, but he seemed alive.

Sammy and Karl knew the two armed

men straight away from the photographs we had been shown. They let them have it. Then they started to get the hostages, most of whom were terrified and shaking, on to the landing and down the stairs. They could be treated later for shock and wounds. Staying alive was the priority now.

Meanwhile, Blue Team members at the back of the embassy were carrying out their part of the assault. They'd blown open the French windows in the basement and rushed into the embassy's library. Then they'd gone into the other basement rooms. Before entering them, they threw in a flash-bang to stun anyone there. Locked doors were blown open with a burst from a 9mm. They found nobody. No hostages. No terrorists.

Above them they could hear shouting and screaming, and explosions and gunfire, so they knew that's where the action was taking place.

Their headsets were jammed with people talking at once, shouting out orders and giving information.

Then Sammy cut through all the talk on the radios.

'Hostages coming down the stairs!'

Chris and I were part of the team to get the hostages out. Just as we'd practised back at Regent's Park Barracks time and again, we joined the others on the stairs, forming a human chain to push the hostages down to the ground floor. While this was happening, others checked through the rooms of the embassy, looking for terrorists or injured or frightened hostages who might be hiding.

As one of the hostages was pushed past me, I felt a spark of recognition. I'd seen that face before. Then I knew where. It had been one of the six faces projected on to the basement wall.

'Terrorist!' I yelled.

Immediately the man turned towards me and opened his coat. I saw that he had grenades strapped to his body and that he was holding one in his hand. If he set it off, the explosion would kill everyone around him. But I couldn't shoot him because a woman hostage was in my line of fire.

'Get out of the way!' I screamed at her as I aimed my gun, ready to fire. But the woman just stood there, terrified.

BRRR-BRRR-BRRR!!!!!!

A burst from a machine-gun on the landing below echoed around the stairwell. The terrorist crumpled, the grenade dropping harmlessly from his hand. I looked down the stairs and saw that it had been Chris who'd fired.

I hurried over to the terrified woman and gave her a shove that sent her stumbling down the stairs to Chris. He grabbed her, helped to steady her, and then passed her on to the next soldier down the stairs.

I kept pushing the hostages along, counting as I did so. I got up to twenty.

Over our radios we began to put together the tally of terrorists killed so far. I'd killed Salim and the one on the second floor. Sammy and Karl had taken out the two who'd been guarding the hostages. Chris had shot the one on the stairs with the hand-grenade. That meant there was one missing. Where was he?

'One terrorist still unaccounted for!' spread the word through our headsets. 'Hostages now out in the garden at the rear of the embassy. Check the rooms of the embassy. Count the hostages.'

I did a quick calculation. There'd been twenty-six hostages at the start. Four had been released. Two were dead, killed by the terrorists. Another was upstairs, badly wounded. That meant nineteen hostages should have gone down the stairs. But twenty people had passed me.

'The missing terrorist is hiding among the hostages!' I shouted into my microphone before hurrying down the stairs.

There was a mad scramble to get to the garden, where the hostages were lying face down on the ground. One by one we checked their faces, looking for the one who was pretending.

'Which one is he?' I yelled at the hostages.

Then Noodle shouted out, 'Got him!'

Noodle and Mucker hauled a young man to his feet and pulled back the hood he had up to hide his identity. He looked terrified, but there was no mistaking who he was – the missing terrorist.

'So you thought you could escape, did you?' said Terry, aiming his gun at him.

The man dropped to his knees, shaking with fear and mumbling in his own language. Probably praying for his life.

'Get up,' shouted Terry. You got lucky this time. The police can deal with you now. Our job is done.'

Chapter 16
THE ELITE

Six days after the siege had begun, our job was over. The hostages had been rescued. Five of the terrorists had been killed. It was time for us to get back to our basement for a debriefing.

It was on the way back there that I realized I had completely forgotten about Chocko ...

'What's happened to Chocko?' I asked.

'On his way to hospital,' said Mucker. 'Didn't you know about him?'

'I saw him get caught up, but I didn't stop to help him,' I admitted. 'Is he OK?'

Mucker explained to me what had happened to Chocko.

As Chocko dangled just above the second-floor balcony, the fire spread from the curtains by the window. Soon the whole window frame was alight and the heat began blistering the skin on his legs. The flames had also gone through his boots to burn his feet. To get away from the fire, Chocko kicked away from the wall. But when he pushed himself away, he swung back into the flames.

The guys on the roof had seen the problem and tried to cut through his rope so that he could drop down to the balcony. Every time they went to cut the rope, Chocko pushed himself away from the wall. If they'd cut the rope then, he would have fallen on to the pavement and not on to the balcony. Falling to the ground would have injured him badly, if not killed him.

It was a desperate situation. Finally, two of Red Team managed to get on to the balcony and prepared to catch Chocko. Up on the roof, they cut through his nylon rope. Amazingly, when Chocko hit the balcony, he pushed away the two blokes waiting to help him.

'Get away from me!' he shouted at them. 'I've got a job to do!'

Next, he plunged through the window, through the flames, to take part in the action inside the embassy, even though his legs were seriously burned. What a man!

When we walked into our basement room in number 15, we found a surprise awaiting us. Someone had provided us with a celebratory treat – four crates of cold bottles of beer stacked up in one corner.

'Hey, look, lads!' called Terry cheerfully, taking a bottle and opening it. 'The Government must have had a whip-round to buy us these!'

We each picked a bottle, opened it, and settled ourselves down in the easy chairs, on the settees, anywhere there was a comfortable space. Not that we actually relaxed. After an action like that the adrenalin is still pumping and it's hard to come down to earth. You feel ready to do a ten-mile run. Especially when it had been a good result, like today.

The TV set was still on and we saw ourselves on the news as the whole event was replayed. There was Blue Team coming over the ramp and blowing out the windows, and most of the first-floor balcony. I saw myself up on the edge of the roof, dressed head to foot in black, ready to abseil down. All the lads cheered as we watched ourselves in action. Suddenly, Colonel Jackson's voice cut through the noise.

'Gentlemen, the Prime Minister,' he announced.

My first thought was that it must be a joke. Then, to my amazement, the Prime Minister walked in, accompanied by a small entourage of people.

'No need to get up,' the Prime Minister said. 'I just came to say what a great job you all did. The country is proud of you. I'm proud of you!'

'For heaven's sake, sit down!' called out Noodle's voice. 'I'm trying to watch myself on the telly and you're blocking my view!'

For a second there was a hush. We all looked at Colonel Jackson, expecting him to shout at Noodle.

But before he could say anything, the Prime Minister, said, 'That man is absolutely right.'

And then the Prime Minister and the rest of the top brass all sat down to watch the action replay.

How amazing is that, I thought to

myself? The Prime Minister of Great Britain, one of the most powerful people in the world, is told to move out of the way by a soldier – and does so. How many other soldiers of any army in the world would say something similar to their leader and get away with it? How many leaders would show the soldier so much respect? But then, the SAS are no ordinary army. We are the élite and as such demanded everyone's respect – even a Prime Minister's.

HISTORICAL NOTE

This book, although fictional, is based on a real event: the siege of the Iranian Embassy in London in 1980. It lasted five days. It began on Wednesday 30 April 1980, when six terrorists took over the embassy, demanding the release of their colleagues from prisons in Iran. The siege ended on Monday 5 May, when the SAS stormed the building.

On the afternoon of the first day of the siege, as soon as the Government learned of the attack, Home Secretary William Whitelaw called a meeting of the Committee of the Cabinet Office in Briefing Room A (COBRA). It was attended by senior members of the Ministry of Defence, the branches of the secret service, and the Director of the SAS. The Prime Minister of Britain, Margaret Thatcher, was not present, but her views were made known to the committee: the terrorists would not be allowed to leave the country. The Government wanted negotiations with the terrorists to continue as long as necessary to bring about a peaceful solution. However, if two or more of the hostages were killed, then the SAS would be sent in to rescue the rest of the hostages and kill the terrorists.

On 5 May one of the hostages, a Press Attaché at the Iranian Embassy, was shot dead. His body was thrown out by the terrorists on to the street in front of the embassy. The terrorists also claimed they had killed a second hostage. When the SAS entered the embassy they did indeed find the body of a second man, the assistant Press Attaché, although it was possible he was killed by the terrorists during the actual assault.

The SAS attack began at 19.27 hours on Monday 5 May and ended at 20.07 hours, forty minutes later. Of the original total of twenty-six hostages, four were released before the assault and two were killed by the terrorists. The embassy's *Chargé d'Affaires* was shot in the face and legs by the terrorists, but he survived. He was among the hostages who were rescued.

The SAS force killed five of the terrorists, including their leader. The terrorist who survived was given a life sentence for manslaughter. At the time of writing, he remains in a British prison.

Injuries were received by the SAS teams. One of the men was shot in the hand. The hood of one of the abseilers caught fire as he descended through the flames at the back of the embassy. His respirator was so badly burned that he took it off and went through the whole attack without a gas mask to protect him from the CS gas being used.

The most seriously injured SAS soldier was trapped on the abseiling rope at the back of the building, and one of his legs was burned badly. Yet, after he had been cut down, he still went ahead with his part in the assault on the embassy. He was awarded the George Medal for this act of courage.

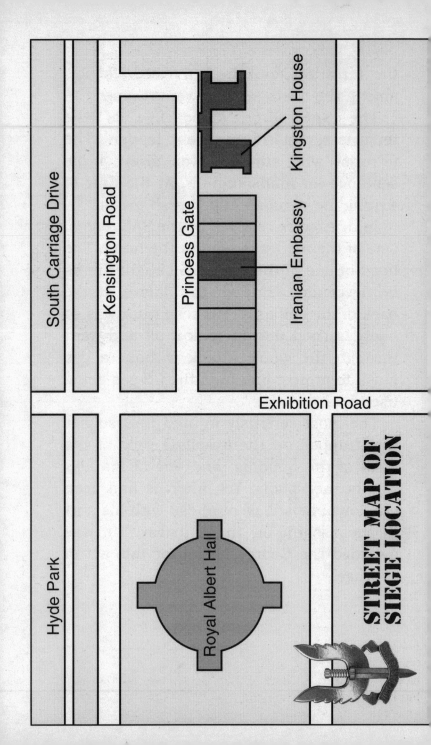

STREET MAP OF SIEGE LOCATION

Hyde Park

South Carriage Drive

Kensington Road

Princess Gate

Royal Albert Hall

Exhibition Road

Iranian Embassy

Kingston House

SAS STORM THE EMBASSY

STAGE ONE – REAR ATTACK

At 7.23 p.m. explosives were lowered into the embassy stairwell from a skylight. The explosion was the signal for the SAS to move in and eight SAS men abseiled down two ropes at the rear of the building. One of the men was entangled in his ropes and so the other men were forced to hack their way into the building rather than use explosives, which may have injured him.

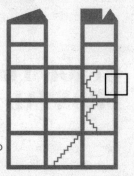

STAGE TWO –
FRONTAL ASSAULT

A second assault team used explosives to blow out
the windows at the front of the embassy. This was
the explosion seen live on television. One of the
hostages was in this room and when the room was
engulfed in fire he had to be hauled to safety on
a neighbouring balcony.

STAGE THREE – PC LOCK'S HEROISM

As the assault began, PC Trevor Lock was with Salim, the leader of the gunmen. When an SAS man appeared at the window, PC Lock prevented him from being shot by tackling the gunman. The SAS burst into the room and shot Salim. PC Lock was awarded the George Cross for his brave actions.

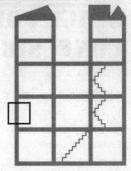

STAGE FOUR – CONFUSION

In the confusion of the explosions, the gunmen opened fire, killing one hostage and injuring two others. The SAS then stormed into the room and shot two of the terrorist gunmen.

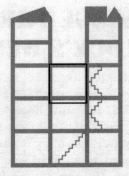

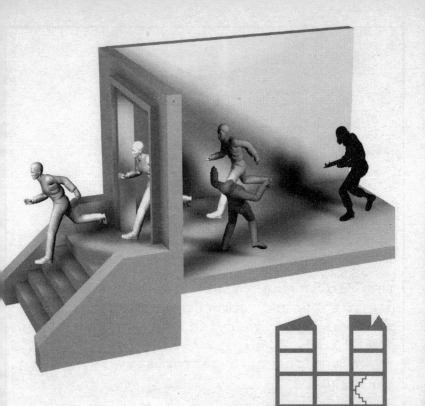

STAGE FIVE - HOSTAGES FREED

The hostages were guided out of the burning building by the SAS. During this process another gunman carrying a grenade was shot dead by the SAS. Once outside, the hostages were taken to waiting ambulances for treatment. The sixth gunman was identified among the hostages and taken away by police.

HOSTAGE RELEASE EQUIPMENT

The following list is the standard equipment and clothing worn by SAS soldiers when carrying out an assault on a building, a ship, a train – an aircraft, any place in which terrorists are holding hostages.

ASSAULT SUIT:
This is a one-piece suit that is worn under body armour. It is designed to offer protection against injury from fire.

BALACLAVA:
This is made of double-jersey knitted black fabric. It provides protection for the face and head against fire. A larger version is also made that fits over a respirator.

ASSAULT GLOVES:
These are made of black Kevlar, a flame-resistant and waterproof fabric.

ASSAULT BELT RIG:
Made of black leather, this is for the SAS soldier's personal weapons and ammunition. It has a pistol holster, a grenade carrier and magazine carriers.

ASSAULT HELMET AND BALLISTIC VISOR:
This is made from polyaramid. It is bullet-proof up to 9mm Geco steel-jacketed ammunition at a velocity of 420 metres per second when fired from a sub-machine gun. It incorporates a radio headset and microphone.

BODY ARMOUR:
It includes ceramic plates which provide protection against high-velocity bullets up to 7.62mm x 51 USM61. The armour is covered in Arvex SNX 574 flame-resistant fabric.

RESPIRATOR:
The CT-12 respirator protects against CS, CR and other gases. It has a rubber face-piece that can be fitted with tinted polycarbonate lenses to provide protection against flash and fragments.

The CT400 radio communications system consists of a combined ear defender and radio headset. It is worn under the balaclava and allows each soldier to be in communication with other members of his team.

Jake, Jerry and I travelled about a 100 metres behind the ridge until we were out of sight of the huts' windows and only fifty metres from the helicopter and the ATV.

We pulled ourselves up over the ridge and dropped into the snow on the other side. Here it was so thin that scrub and rock poked through.

'No sense crawling over this lot,' muttered Jerry.

I nodded.

'Let's go,' I said.

Crouching low, the three of us ran at speed, covering the distance to the Alouette and the ATV as quickly as possible. As we neared the helicopter I was already opening my bag with one hand and taking out the plastic explosive. While Jerry dropped to a firing position behind the helicopter, his gun trained on the huts, I set to work.

I packed some of the explosive at the rear of the chopper, just by the tail rotor. When I was sure it was fixed securely, I pushed the remote-controlled detonator into the mass of plastic. Then I moved to the belly of the Alouette, underneath where the fuel tank would be. Once more I moulded the plastic explosive into shape, packed it against the fuselage and pushed the thin detonator into it. I shot a quick glance across to the ATV. I saw Jake hauling himself out from beneath it. He gave a thumbs up.

'Right,' I hissed at Jerry. 'That's it. We're go.'

Jerry nodded and we all turned to head back towards the ice-ridge. Just then, I heard a door slam open.

Immediately, we threw ourselves flat on the ground, turning as we did so towards the sound, hoping we hadn't been seen.

We had.

There was a shout of 'Atacar!', Spanish for 'Attack!'. Next a Guantinian soldier opened up from the open door. Bullets smacked into the ground near us, throwing chips of rocks and ice up into our faces.

Don't let them hit the explosives! I prayed silently.

Jerry let off a burst from his rifle towards the enemy soldier, and we heard the door slam shut.

Looking towards the huts, I saw that windows were being opened and rifle-barrels were being poked through them.

'Time to go!' said Jerry.

He fired one last burst. Jake and I did the same and then we ran zigzag fashion towards the ice-ridge, bullets flying all around us, even plucking at our clothes.

BRR-BRRR-BRRR!!!!!

Mack opened fire from his position behind the ridge. There was the sound of glass shattering as he shot out windows in the huts. The enemy soldiers stopped firing and they ducked away from the windows, giving me, Jake and Jerry time to complete our dash to the ridge and hurl ourselves over it.

'OK!' I shouted at Mack. 'Blow the plastic!'

'You're sure you're not still too close to it?' laughed Mack.

'Just blow it!' I yelled.

'After all, I suppose they know we're here now!' grinned Jerry.

The air was filled with the roar of explosions – two from the heli-pad, one from the ATV. Jake had set his plastic explosives underneath the traction mechanism on the ATV. As Mack detonated it, the caterpillar tracks were blown out, curling up like broken elastic-bands, with bits of metal flying everywhere.

On the helicopter, the explosive at the tail end blew off the rear rotor. But the explosion of the fuel tank was truely spectacular. It was so huge that for a second I thought we were going to be engulfed in it. There was a massive WHOOOMPPP!! and a ball of red and white flame shot out from the chopper. Then it seemed to rise up into the air as the fuel tank went up. As it crashed down it began to crumple and fall apart in a tangle of twisted metal and thick black oily smoke.

Mack kept up sporadic firing at the huts to keep the Guantinians at bay while we ran along behind the ice-ridge, crouching low.

'One to us,' I said. 'Well done, Mack.'

From the huts came a burst of gunfire

as someone braved Mack's fire. The bullets skimmed through the air just above our heads.

'Time to go,' said Jerry.

'We're still carrying plastic explosive in this bag,' said Mack. 'I don't fancy being around if one of them hits that.'

'Let's give them something to think about,' said Jake.

He pulled out a grenade, took out the pin, then tossed it towards the hut where the firing was coming from. The grenade rolled to a stop just beneath an open window.

'When that goes off, with luck they'll think we're firing mortars at them and get away from the windows.'

The gunfire continued. We counted down. 6 ... 5 ... 4 ... 3 ... 2 ... 1 ...

Boooooom!!!

As the grenade went off, the firing stopped abruptly.

'Let's go!' snapped Mack.

We were already running, hauling our weapons and bags with us. Every few steps two of us turned and fired off a burst towards the huts, covering the other pair as they ran on ahead. Soon the four of us were out of range of the enemy's small-arms weapons. If they wanted to chase us with bigger weapons, they'd have to come out of the huts to do it.

We regrouped with the rest of the squad.

'Mission accomplished,' I said to Captain Wilson. 'The chopper and the ATV both out of action.'

'And pretty thoroughly, by the sound of it!' grinned Wilson. 'Good job. Right, my guess is that all that action will have the Guantinians at Solsborg bleating for help from the major force on their ships docked at Troon.'

'Do you think they'll move the ship along the coast to Solsborg?' I asked.

Wilson mulled it over.

'They might send the frigate, but I doubt if they'll move the ice-breaker,' he said at last. 'It secures the base at Troon. Remember, there's no base for them ashore and no proper cover. So the ice-breaker is probably their HQ. I think they'll send major reinforcements overland to Solsborg – with ATVs, heavy weapons, the lot. And on the way they'll be looking for us. If I'm right, it's a good opportunity to free the prisoners on the ice-breaker, if that's where they are.'

'And if you're wrong?' queried Jake.

Wilson grinned.

'We'll end up in big trouble. Really big trouble,' he said.

w.puffin.co.uk.www.puffin.co.uk.www.puffin.co.uk

okinfo.competitions.news.games.sneakpreviews

w.puffin.co.uk.www.puffin.co.uk.www.puffin.co.uk

venture.bestsellers.fun.coollinks.freestuff

w.puffin.co.uk.www.puffin.co.uk.www.puffin.co.uk

plore.yourshout.awards.toptips.authorinfo

w.puffin.co.uk.www.puffin.co.uk.www.puffin.co.uk

eatbooks.greatbooks.greatbooks.greatbooks

w.puffin.co.uk.www.puffin.co.uk.www.puffin.co.uk

views.poems.jokes.authorevents.audioclips

w.puffin.co.uk.www.puffin.co.uk.www.puffin.co.uk

erviews.e-mailupdates.bookinfo.competitions.news

www.puffin.co.uk

mes.sneakpreviews.adventure.bestsellers.fun

w.puffin.co.uk.www.puffin.co.uk.www.puffin.co.uk

okinfo.competitions.news.games.sneakpreviews

w.puffin.co.uk.www.puffin.co.uk.www.puffin.co.uk

venture.bestsellers.fun.coollinks.freestuff

w.puffin.co.uk.www.puffin.co.uk.www.puffin.co.uk

plore.yourshout.awards.toptips.authorinfo

w.puffin.co.uk.www.puffin.co.uk.www.puffin.co.uk

eatbooks.greatbooks.greatbooks.greatbooks

w.puffin.co.uk.www.puffin.co.uk.www.puffin.co.uk

views.poems.jokes.authorevents.audioclips

w.puffin.co.uk.www.puffin.co.uk.www.puffin.co.uk

Read more in Puffin

For complete information about books available from Puffin – and Penguin – and how to
order them, contact us at the appropriate address below. Please note that for copyright
reasons the selection of books varies from country to country.

www.puffin.co.uk

In the United Kingdom: Please write to Dept EP, Penguin Books Ltd,
Bath Road, Harmondsworth, West Drayton, Middlesex UB7 ODA

In the United States: Please write to Penguin Putnam Inc., P.O. Box 12289,
Dept B, Newark, New Jersey 07101–5289 or call 1–800–788–6262

In Canada: Please write to Penguin Books Canada Ltd,
10 Alcorn Avenue, Suite 300, Toronto, Ontario M4V 3B2

In Australia: Please write to Penguin Books Australia Ltd,
P.O. Box 257, Ringwood, Victoria 3134

In New Zealand: Please write to Penguin Books (NZ) Ltd,
Private Bag 102902, North Shore Mail Centre, Auckland 10

In India: Please write to Penguin Books India Pvt Ltd,
11 Panscheel Shopping Centre, Panscheel Park, New Delhi 110 017

In the Netherlands: Please write to Penguin Books Netherlands bv,
Postbus 3507, NL–1001 AH Amsterdam

In Germany: Please write to Penguin Books Deutschland GmbH,
Metzlerstrasse 26, 60594 Frankfurt am Main

In Spain: Please write to Penguin Books S. A., Bravo Murillo 19,
1° B, 28015 Madrid

In Italy: Please write to Penguin Italia s.r.l.,
Via Felice Casati 20, I–20124 Milano

In France: Please write to Penguin France S. A.,
17 rue Lejeune, F–31000 Toulouse

In Japan: Please write to Penguin Books Japan, Ishikiribashi Building,
2–5–4, Suido, Bunkyo-ku, Tokyo 112

In South Africa: Please write to Longman Penguin Southern Africa (Pty) Ltd,
Private Bag X08, Bertsham 2013